The Devil's

TRIANGLE

JESSICA
BENOIST-YOUNG

THE DEVIL'S TRIANGLE
Copyright © 2017 by Jessica Benoist-Young.

This book is a work of fiction. Names, characters, businesses, organizations, places, events and incidents either are the product of the author's imagination or are used fictitiously. Any resemblance to actual persons, living or dead, events, or locales is entirely coincidental.

For information:
http://www.jessicabenoistyoung.com

Book Cover and design by Jessica Benoist-Young

First Edition: September 2017

Thanks to my family, who keeps laughing at me just enough to convince me I'm funny.

CHAPTER 1

DON'T SAY THAT

"This is the third time in a month you've come in here and bought some cheap-ass piece of furniture, Mickey. Your parties getting out of control or something?"

Tony looked at me with raised eyebrows over his dollar store reading glasses as he took my five dollars and stuffed them in the cash register.

"It's for therapy," I said casually, watching as he immediately pumped hand sanitizer into his palm and slathered it all over his hands after touching my dollar bills.

Couldn't say I blamed him...

"I don't get why you need cheap end tables and bookshelves for therapy, Mickey," he said, shaking his head. "You go to some sort of weirdo hippie therapist? Like makes you go skinny dipping and does the essential oils and shit?"

"Okay, first of all, Tony, please tell me you have never had a therapist that made you go skinny dipping," I groaned. Before he could open his mouth, I held my hands out in front of me to stop him. "Actually, don't answer that, I don't want to know. Secondly, essential oils work, okay? We have been through this."

"Then why d'you need therapy?" he asked, crossing his arm.

"Because I can't afford the essential oil that keeps me from wanting to kill people, Tony," I replied, grabbing up the rickety, coral-painted wicker end table I had just shelled out a venti iced latte's amount of money for.

"Rough day?" Tony asked, cocking his head, an expression of genuine concern on his forty-something face.

"Try year," I sighed.

"Is it guy stuff? Family stuff? Work stuff?"

"Well, seeing as I have no *guy* and no family left, and work is pretty much all I do, I think it's work."

"That reminds me, I've been meanin' to come see ya."

I rolled my eyes and dropped the end table back to the floor.

"Please don't say that."

"What? I have been."

"I don't want you to, Tony," I said, more curtly than intended, but it was true. "If I get a nice job at a coffee shop or a clothing store you can come see me all you want. And you can come see me now, but just don't tell me about."

"Why not? I was tryin' to be polite."

"It's weird, Tony. We are neighbors. I've shopped at your thrift store for years...I don't want to think about you seeing my tits."

"I've seen a lot of tits in my life, Mickey," he chuckled, "If that makes you feel any better."

"Strangely, it does..." I muttered, scrunching my face in mild disgust.

"If you're so unhappy at work—and I still don't see how a five dollar wicker end table plays into this but—maybe you should start lookin', y'know, for another job?"

"Trust me, I have looked, but there isn't much out there with better pay at entry level right now. I'm still paying student loans so it's not like going *back* to school is a viable option right now. And I have a perfectly good degree! I just...failed, I guess."

"You aren't doing the wedding photography gigs anymore?" Tony asked.

"God, no. It was so awkward. I recognized almost all of the grooms, and they usually recognized me," I explained. "Not to mention the groomsmen, and even a few of the brides."

Tony laughed his bellowing, wheezy laugh. "I can imagine. Well, I will keep my eyes and ears open in case anybody I know is hiring for a job that pays better than stripping."

I didn't even bother looking around the store to see if there was anyone else in it (I had checked when I came in and there were two). Maybe when I first started working at the strip club, I would have cared about Tony declaring my 'profession' in a store full of strangers, but now...well, it was a small neighborhood and I had lived here for four years, and been a stripper for half of that, so by now everyone knew.

And Tony meant well. Tony always meant well. He lived in my apartment building and, in addition to owning the neighborhood thrift and consignment store, he was the emergency handyman for our building. We had first met when my dishwasher crapped out within a month of moving into my place, flooding my kitchen floor in the middle of the night.

He was like an uncle to me at this point—other than the fact he had seen me in nothing but a thong once or twice. He never judged me, though he certainly was old-fashioned enough to be concerned that I was a single woman in her twenties living alone in a rough neighborhood in St. Louis. He would never admit it, because he knew I'd give him a lecture on sexism, but he was protective. He had a daughter about the same age as me who had moved to Brooklyn for college and stayed there, and I had always sort of assumed I was an object of projection for him. He could be protective of me, supportive of me and it feel like he was taking care of and looking out for his daughter, as well.

"Oh, sorry, Mickey," he apologized. "*Exotic dancer.*"

I laughed. "It's fine, Tony. But I better get going. I still need to deal with this *therapy* session and eat dinner before work."

I picked up the ugly end table and, with a short salute, turned and headed out of the thrift store.

"I still don't understand why you need an end table for therapy!" he called after me.

"Someday I'll show ya!"

Goggles on, but no gloves—I liked the way it felt against my pole blisters—I gripped the handle of the sledgehammer, my muscles tensing as I lifted it and prepared to bring it down upon its victim. The secondhand end table shattered with an orchestra of satisfying smashes and splinters, spraying shards of wicker like coral porcupine quills across the tarp I had laid under it on the roof of my apartment building.

The first blow decimated the top and split the table in two, but the legs were still intact. I hauled the sledge hammer up again, with an aching protest from my deltoids, and drove it down once more. A shower of wicker covered the tarp, sounding exactly like heavy rain.

My heart pounded, sweat dripped down the sides of my face and pooled between my boobs in my sports bra. I propped my sledgehammer against the wall, grabbed my beer, which was sweating about as much as I was, and took a refreshing swig as I surveyed the scene.

I shook my head and clicked my tongue, then spoke out loud to absolutely no one. "Wood is much better. Especially good construction wooden furniture. A longer and more gratifying experience. I should have gone for that end table with the light attached, but I was afraid the lamp would get in the way. Lesson learned."

In another voice, I pretended to be my beer: "You know, you could smash dishes like normal people."

"Quiet, beer, nobody asked you," I said in my regular voice and took a long drink. "Besides, the key here is the sledgehammer. Throwing a few dishes would have the stress relieving affects from breaking shit, sure, but I wouldn't feel the soreness from it afterward—the blisters, the muscle ache."

In my beer voice: "Ooooohhhh, you're a masochist."

"You know, you're a tasty drink, but I don't have to listen to your shit," I muttered in my normal voice, a smirk pulling at my lips. "See? This is why I needed a *wooden* table—the wooden table would have taken three or four times as long and I wouldn't be standing here talking to my beer!"

"Good point," in beer voice. "That bookcase was the best, wasn't it," beer voice said with a wistful sigh.

"God, it really fucking was," I purred. "Wait, that wasn't you—that was a different beer."

"We were from the same brewery," beer voice said. "It's like a shared consciousness thing."

"I see," I nodded at the beer and raised my eyebrows in consideration. "I am actually losing it, aren't I?"

Beer voice said "Yes."

"That's what I thought," I sighed. "I don't know how much longer I can do this."

"What do you wanna do?" beer voice asked.

"I want to move to Africa."

"And do what, Mickey?"

"Beer, you are really nosy—and really hoppy, did you know that? You are delicious. Does the 'I' in IPA stand for 'I love drinking you'?"

"You know it doesn't. Don't change the subject."

"I don't know, beer, I just want to get as far away from this type of life as I can. I want to ride camels and take beautiful photos and live somewhere colorful and not eat fast food all the time."

"And not get Ebola."

"Well, that goes without saying."

I swirled the last few ounces of the beer around the bottom of the condensation-covered can.

"I guess I should clean this up," I mumbled.

"Yes, you should, and you should finish me so you'll quit talking to me like a crazy person," beer voice quipped.

"Oh, look who's the masochist now!" I replied, holding the beer in front of my face. "If you insist, beer." Dramatically, I threw my head back and drained the remainder of the beer, smacking my lips and exhaling sharply.

With a dejected sigh, I started to roll up the tarp, making sure all the little pieces of pinkish wicker were contained in it, and scooped the tarp up in my arms, walking it to the dumpster and shaking the deconstructed end table out into its gaping metallic brown mouth.

It was time to get ready for work. And the 'therapy session' had been underwhelming. *Maybe beer was right—maybe I should go grab some dishes and smash the fuck out of them,* I thought. The cleanup would be worse. *Maybe I could drop the dishes from the roof right in front of or behind people walking by...?*

Jesus fucking Christ, what the fuck is wrong with me?

If I still had any beer left, I would have said it out loud.

Tony was out of small furniture items after the wicker table I had just destroyed, and the end table with the lamp attached. Unless he got some good donations or consignment items soon, I would have to come up with something else to help me release my anger and frustration.

If there was more kicking or punching things in yoga, I would have stuck with that. And if it weren't so expensive to have a membership to the boxing gym, I would probably kick and punch things. People things, which I figured would help a *lot*.

People were the problem here. The people I worked with, the people who came to my work, people in general...people made me so fucking angry all the time. The only people I liked anymore were Tony and the guys that ran the cronut food truck that parked across the street from the strip club on the weekends.

If it were the weekend, I would *at least* have the food truck to look forward to. But it was a fucking Wednesday. The worst day of the week...

Back in my apartment, tarp and sledgehammer cradled in my arms then promptly dumped on the floor by the coat hooks, I made a beeline for the fridge and grabbed another beer. The crack and hiss when I opened it was almost as satisfying and refreshing as the drink itself.

"Seriously, why do people still think its funny to say 'It's hump day!' at all, let alone to a stripper?" I asked the new beer.

"People aren't funny, Mickey," new beer said. New beer had the same voice as old beer, because I really wasn't good at voices.

I groaned as I took new beer to the shower. "You can say that again."

CHAPTER 2

THE GAP BETWEEN WHERE YOU ARE...

Thumping bass greeted me with the familiar reverberation in my chest as I entered SugarLand through the front door, walking straight to the bar.

"How many beers have you had, Martin?" my boss, Mitch, asked with scrunched eyebrows as I approached.

"Two," I answered. "And I'm forty minutes early, which is plenty of time to finish a third."

He sighed and pulled a bottle out of the bar fridge and pried the top off for me, my ears delighting in the comforting rasp of escaping air. "I told you to come in the back door."

"That's what she said!" the man sitting at the bar next to me slurred, then slapped his hand on the bar top several times while engaging in silent hysterical laughter.

I hate this place, I thought to myself, giving the obviously drunk man a warning side-eyed glare as he grabbed my elbow in his laughing fit. He removed his hand, gradually composed himself, and went back to his beer, and when I looked back, Mitch was fixing a disapproving stare on me.

"Then I wouldn't get to see you, Mitch," I said with a grin.

"This is what you do!" he griped, holding his hands out in exasperation toward the drunk guy.

"What? What do I do?"

"You scare people."

"I don't—"

"You scare *men.*"

I snorted a laugh through my nose. "Well...it's not like that's difficult.

I have a vagina."

"See? That. That...attitude toward the customers. *Customers*, Mickey. Like, the people who pay your wages?"

"Wait, are you trying to tell me that I not only have to do this degrading shit for germ-infested pocket change, but I have to enjoy it, too?" I chuckled with the beer bottle resting on my lips, preparing for a nice refreshing swig.

"No, I'm not saying that," Mitch said, shaking his head and sighing. "I'm just saying you shouldn't hang out up here. Because you're not very nice."

I choked on my beer as a deep laugh took momentary control of my throat. "Nice?" I echoed, cocking my head and raising my eyebrows.

"You're taunting me with your fucking face, Martin," Mitch pointed out, gesturing at me in frustration. "That's not something nice people do."

"I *can* be a nice person, Mitch," I said. "It just requires a level of energy I don't feel I should spend on drunken horndogs or the population of St. Louis as a whole. Efficiency, Mitchie. If I don't spend the energy there, I can spend it elsewhere."

"Like on what?" he retorted with an eye roll.

"On perfecting my pole spins, or binging 'Cheers' on Netflix, or deeply loathing myself for hours at a time while I check the cost of living in Azerbaijan. Again."

"Oh my God, Mick, get outta here before you freak people out. Take your beer. Go get ready—go. Please."

Sliding my bottle off the bar, I gave him a wink and strolled away from the bar toward the dressing room. A monotone, unenthused concert of ritualistic greetings sounded upon my entry. None of us were excited to see any of the others. None of us were excited to be there at all, unless somebody had done a bunch of blow before or upon arrival—which wasn't uncommon.

My vice of choice was beer, and always had been. It came with the side effects of bringing out my sarcastic side—which apparently made me come across as 'not very nice'— and adding a lot of carb-laden calories to my daily intake, but if this job was good for anything other than money, it was the workout.

We laughed regularly about the rich women in the fancy gyms downtown, taking pole dance fitness classes to get ripped abs and 'bring out their inner sexy'. If any of them had ever actually set foot in a strip club, they probably wouldn't associate that shiny pole in their swanky gym with sexy.

I certainly didn't think there was anything sexy about it. It was all a farce. A show, and not a good one. It was as routine for everyone involved as an actual trip to the gym, but as banal as getting on the treadmill, or fumbling through the weight machines that nobody besides bodybuilders and trainers really knew how to use. Everyone who came to a gentleman's club was choosing to take part in a custom that was awkward at best, and degrading at worst, but so ordinary and commonplace in pop culture, we all just kept engaging in the libertine theatrics of it without question.

Did any of them—those sweaty, eager men who sat on smelly, crappy sofas and drank syrupy, overpriced cocktails—know why they were here, other than because it was such an accessible tradition to participate in? Get drunk, see tits, cat call, throw money. Repeat with new tits and new drinks.

It was like church, but instead of worshipping a deity, they were worshipping the opportunity to see breasts. As someone who'd had breasts for over a decade, I thought it was a pretty silly thing to worship. Not to say I didn't like them, but I hadn't ever seen a pair that compelled me to hang out in the stank and squalor of a Midwestern strip joint and give monetary reward to their owner.

One of the girls coming in from the afternoon shift broke my internal ramblings with her high-pitched squeal of an announcement. "Good crowd today!"

I chuckled in my throat. Anytime someone said there was a 'good crowd' it really meant a rowdy, drunken, libidinous crowd that had lost control of their bodies and wallets.

"A fraternity house," she clarified, a hint of triumph that she'd tamed the young and undiscerning loins of college students in her chirpy voice.

"Fuck my life," I grumbled.

"What's the deal? They're probably rich," said Jenny, one of the girls who was hired around the same time as me.

"Exactly, so they're entitled, and think their money justifies shitty behavior," I replied.

"Well, if you're so fucking prurient, don't take their money," Jenny teased.

"That's...Jenny, that's not what that means. Prurient means sexy. Raunchy."

"Well, then what word am I thinking of," she asked, tilting her head toward her shoulder.

"I have no fucking idea," I chuckled as I pulled on my light-up platform shoes. "Prudent?"

"I don't know, maybe," she sighed with a shrug. "Anyways, you've been a judgy bitch lately, especially for someone who has no problem taking home the cash afterward."

"You're right," I said. "On top of everything else to love about it, this job is making me a raging hypocrite! It's also making me destroy furniture and talk to my beer."

"What are you talking about?" Jenny asked, her heavily made-up face twisting in confusion.

"Nothing." I slammed my locker shut and took a deep breath. "Now, let's go see how long it takes these *prurient* frat boys to run out of money."

The first hour or so wasn't terrible—the fraternity brothers kept their attention on Jenny and Molly, the sweet-looking blondes, while I entertained some lonely regulars who generally stayed tame and paid decently. One was a friend of Mitch's and always tried to chit-chat about the weather and sports, which I humored with bland answers and the sweetest smile I could muster as it made him more generous with his cash.

But as the night went on and the crowd thinned out, and the liquor started to take its inevitable toll, they started to roam the club looking for their next victims...

The skin of my palms burned and stung. The blisters that had been made worse from gripping the sledgehammer earlier that day rubbed against the metal of the pole as I hoisted all my weight off the floor into a split straddle.

"Let's find one with a thigh gap," I heard one of the wandering frat boys say.

My grip threatened to falter as the pain of the blistered skin against the smooth rod turned from a sting to a sear, as if I'd put both my hands on a black car in hundred-degree sun. I tried my best to ignore them—if I didn't act like I wanted them to come toward me, maybe they would be deterred—and doubled my focus on keeping my hold through the rest of the song.

"What about this one?" the guy next to him asked.

Fuck. They were pointing at me.

"Didn't your mother ever teach you it's rude to point?" I muttered, rolling my eyes.

"Ooh, a feisty one!" the first one squealed with delight.

"She does have red hair," said the second. "Does the—"

"The curtains are burgundy and obviously dyed, you idiot," I cut him off before he could finish the ridiculous, lewd question.

He giggled into his cocktail. "I don't know your kink."

"Hey, do you have a thigh gap?" the other piped up. "Put your feet on the ground—stand up! Let's see."

"C'mon, Merlot," the second frat boy added with a smirk, "there's a fifty for you if you do."

"If I stand up, or if I have a thigh gap?" I spat in disgust.

"I am not giving you fifty bucks for putting your feet on the floor," he scoffed.

"I wouldn't give her fifty bucks for anything," the first one chortled. "She definitely has a boob gap. Nowhere for me to put my big bills." He nudged his friend with his elbow.

"What are you, like, twenty-one *today*?!" I teased. "How many boobs have you seen that you didn't have to pay or rufie someone to see?"

I watched in profound amusement as he actually considered the question, his eyes shifting up toward the ceiling as he seemed to be counting boobs in his head.

"Five," he finally answered confidently.

"Someone only showed you one?" I laughed, so hard that my grip finally slipped and I lost the strength to hold myself up anymore. I put my feet down and doubled over with laughter.

"No, I mean five people showed me their boobs," he rebutted.

"She does!" the second one elated. "She does have a thigh gap!"

I snapped up from my bent over position and glared at him.

"Alright, where do you want your fifty?" he asked, raising his eyebrows at me suggestively.

"Put it towards a women's studies class next semester," I snapped. "How about that?"

He stalked a few more steps toward the stage until he was leaning right up against it with his hands splayed on either side of him. "I'm studying women right now, Merlot," he purred.

I crouched down in front of him and our eyes were level, and he instinctively angled his head toward mine. "You are studying bodies. Not women."

He smirked. "If you are offering yourself for research, I could be persuaded to partake in some women's studies."

I tilted my head and narrowed my eyes at him. "I am neither a prostitute, nor am I flirting with you, so why exactly are you propositioning me?"

"C'mon, Merlot," he murmured, "just having a bit of fun." He leaned even farther forward over the stage until his face was only an inch from mine, and I jerked back instinctively, thinking he was going to try to kiss me. Then I felt the smooth paper bill against the skin of my hip as he tucked it into my G-string. "I mean, there's a VIP room here, right?" he added in what I assumed was the most seductive tone he could muster as he raised his eyebrows at me again.

I dropped forward onto my hands and knees and dropped my lips to his earlobe. "Of course there is," I whispered, and his entire body shuddered.

I slinked off the stage and grabbed his hand, leading him to the 'VIP room'. We slipped through the beaded curtain and I felt his hand go sweaty in mine, and my blisters shrieked in protest at the introduction of moisture. I led him to an open chair—of which there were many as we rarely utilized the semi-private room—and forcefully sat him down in it. A goofy grin consumed his boyish face.

Swaying and snaking my body, I moved in on him. He tensed and dropped his head back as I ran my hands down his solid arms. He squirmed as my fingers found the button and zipper of his jeans. He hummed in his throat and breathed heavily as I pulled the jeans down and slipped them over his sandaled feet. He moaned in approval as I ripped open the front of his sweaty, button up shirt.

Without a word, I tucked the fifty dollar bill into his boxers, which were noticeably tented at the front.

"Close your eyes," I whispered in his ear, and he did as told without hesitation.

Jeans in one hand, I pulled the fire alarm with the other hand as I left the room through the beaded curtain. The lights throughout the building flicked on to their full strength, and everyone squinted, and a deafening blare like a broken trombone filled the room.

Mitch rushed up to me, his face tight against the bright lights and earsplitting honks and whoops of the alarm.

"What happened—where is the fire?" he barked in a panic.

"You should go ask the hot young stripper in the VIP room," I said.

"What did you do, Martin?" Mitch snapped, his volume considerable to be heard over the alarm system.

"I just wanted to humiliate him," I replied with facetious innocence.

"But I didn't start a fire, don't worry."

"What the hell is your problem lately?"

"My problem? My problem is that I hate this job and I would literally sell my soul to Satan himself not to have to do it anymore!" I shouted in exasperation.

"If you hate it, just quit! You're fucking with my business by bringing your pent up shit in here and taking it out on everyone."

I bit my lip and dropped my head to stare at the carpet. I wanted to quit, but I couldn't...not until I found another job at least.

"Mickey," Mitch sighed and shook his head, "maybe you should take a few days off. And go home, now. Please...just go home."

Without protest, I went to the dressing room where I endured glares from the other girls, put my clothes on, and went home.

CHAPTER 3

...AND WHERE YOU WANT TO BE

I spent the next few days searching for jobs, but, besides

waiting tables, there was nothing available that I was qualified for—and

certainly nothing that would pay better than working at SugarLand. I also

had no idea what Mitch meant by 'a few days', and I was way too stubborn

to call and ask. Waiting for him to call was just about to drive me batty,

though. I had already gone down to Tony's Secondhand Shoppe and bought the sturdy end table with the lamp attached and smashed the shit out of that the day after the fire alarm incident.

The lamp was both satisfying and an issue. Tony had left a light bulb in it, and the tinkling, tinny shatter of its thin glass brought inexplicable joy to my ears. A new sound of destruction to add to the symphony of demolition, its distinctive ring in soprano octave filling a vacant seat in the orchestra. But, the metal of the lamp never yielded to my attempts with the sledgehammer. It was thin and hard to hit with precision, and when I did make contact, it would bend at the point of impact, creaking and groaning its arguments to being hammered in such a manner—but it never snapped or shattered, never scattered into a thousand pieces like wood or wicker or clay or glass.

It was unfinished. It felt unfinished, uncertain, open-ended to me, like a breakup where not all words were said or feelings resolved. It was still up there on the roof, a few remaining pieces of splintered wood clinging to it, and I was probably going to get in trouble with the landlord for not cleaning it up if anyone found it and knew I was up there.

What did I want from it? Just for it to shatter into pieces? To hear what sound it made when it finally broke?

I walked up to the roof and stared at it while sipping my second cup of coffee, lingering on its many bends, how they jutted out and seemed to change color. Remembering various crafts and school projects from childhood, I recalled the trusted technique for snapping wire without scissors. Back and forth...bend it one way, then the opposite way at the same point. Pipe cleaners and silk greenery stems...back and forth, until it breaks.

After carefully setting my coffee cup on the ledge, I knelt down next to the long metal rod that use to be a lamp that used to be attached to an end table. Grabbing it with a hand on either side of a prominent bend, I yanked it back toward me the opposite direction. It whined and cried, and continued its whiny noises as I squeezed my arms and bent it back the original directions.

"Who the fuck made this lamp?" I grunted as my muscles went hot with fatigue. "This is some strong ass metal for the fucking seventies—"

SNAP!

The metallic rupture echoed in the air like a firecracker. I bit my lip and closed my eyes and let it fill my ears.

My serenity was interrupted by a sound that made me jump, even though I had been waiting for it, anticipating it for days—my phone. I whipped it out of my back pocket and, as I suspected, it was Mitch.

I answered: "Hey, Mitch."

"Martin, lunch shift is about to start," Mitch said, his voice rich with excitement and enthusiasm. "I need you here!"

"I-I don't work lunch," I sputtered.

"Just get in here!" he repeated, this time more urgent. "ASAP!"

And he hung up before I could respond.

Confusion hovered over me like one of those cartoon rain clouds as I stood and grabbed my coffee from the ledge, then wandered back to my apartment two floors down from the fifth floor roof. I had already showered and dressed and even put on makeup, so all I needed was shoes and my bag, which I slipped on and grabbed off the coat hook by the door before heading down to my car in the basement garage.

While I drove to SugarLand, I mulled over this urgency to have me work lunch. The shift provided decidedly less tips and thus, usually reserved for newer hires with less experience. Was he easing me back in after my fire alarm offense? Was I still being punished?

Why would he sound so damn happy while telling me that I'm getting the shitty shift after a three-day suspension? None of it made any sense.

And it made even less sense when I pulled into my normal parking spot in front of SugarLand, but SugarLand wasn't there...

"Mitch, what the fuck is this—what is going on?!"

"This is Pizza Pie Palace!" A red t-shirt flew at my face and I caught it with one hand. "That's yours. A small right?"

"Right...I—Mitch, I don't understand," I uttered in shock. "Four days ago, this was a strip club. And now it's a pizza joint? H-how did you—"

Mitch happily worked a blob of pizza dough on the prep counter in the new kitchen—bright white counter tops surrounding a wood-fire oven and open to the dining area, where one table was occupied by two very confused looking businessmen. "My buddy, the lawyer—remember Robby?—Robby called me and said they just found a will for my uncle Gerald and he left me a huge inheritance. *But*, I could only claim the inheritance if I used a portion of the money to start a restaurant."

"That...sounds oddly specific," I muttered.

"I think this was all kismet, Mick," Mitch said, nodding to himself, and then to me. "I really do. You know, kismet? It was meant to be."

"I know what kismet means, Mitch."

"Of course you do," he chuckled and pointed a flour-covered finger at me with a grin. "Because you're smart. And that's part of this. I went home after the fire alarm thing thinking 'gee, if my smartest and best employee is this unhappy, why am I doing this? Is this really the business I want to be in?' And the next morning, Robby called. Kismet."

"Kismet..." I echoed.

"So, what do you think?" he asked, his smile wide, revealing the gold tooth toward the back that I always forgot he had.

I looked around the place, drinking in as many details as possible in my state of confusion. There were a substantial number of tables in the dining area, each covered with a cheap vinyl red-checkered table cloth, which I normally loathed but somehow it worked in the space. The walls that had been black and strewn with string lighting were now a fresh, clean white with a thick red stripe that ran horizontal around the room, just above table height. Black and white pictures of St. Louis mobsters and 1920s speakeasies and Model T Fords were arranged in surprisingly aesthetic clusters on the wall, and little shelves with fake grapes and large bottles of Chianti filled the spaces between them. Brand new black tile flooring, so shiny I could see my reflection in it, had replaced the dingy, stain-ridden carpet.

The stages were gone, the poles and mirrors were gone, the sofas were gone. What was once the rarely used VIP room where I had stranded the obnoxious frat boy was now a party room for birthdays or work functions that featured a Foosball table, a pinball machine, and a classic Galaga arcade game.

"Speechless, right?" Mitch laughed.

"Actually, yes," I said in awe. "How did you do all this in just a few days?"

"I found a great contractor—I mean *great*. Worked all day and all night. I swear sometimes I would come back in the morning and wouldn't believe how much he and his crew had gotten done. Like fucking magic," he explained. He tossed an array of toppings and cheese on his finalized crust. "Ah, Mickey! I'm so happy! This is the happiest I've ever been! It's like my uncle Gerald knew what would make me happy. Like he was watching out for me."

"Were you close?" I asked.

"Never met him," Mitch answered with a shrug.

I laughed softly to myself, but he didn't hear me as he had taken to whistling with the Frank Sinatra tune that filled the room, a nice break from the thumping bass of club music that had reverberated through these walls not long before.

"Get your shirt on, Martin," Mitch urged. "I took an ad out for a Grand Opening lunch special and I need you back here in the kitchen. Grab an apron, too."

"I don't know anything about making pizza," I objected as I pulled the t-shirt over my tank top and walked around behind the counter.

"That's why you're on oven and slicing duty for today. And you may need to jump up front to help the hostess," he instructed. "And you should go out and greet people when you get a chance."

"Geez, Mitch, how much shit do you want me to do?" I laughed as I slipped an apron over my head and tied its strings behind my back.

"Everything. All of it," he answered. "You're my manager, Michaela Martin. If you want it."

I stared at him in shocked silence for several moments before I was able to gather my thoughts into intelligible words. "Um, what does that pay?" I asked as casually as possible, accentuating my attempt at nonchalance by popping a slice of pepperoni in my mouth.

"Forty-five thousand and benefits? Annual raises, of course," Mitch offered.

I gasped and choked on the pepperoni, coughing until it was clear of my airway. I nodded fervently through the hacking and asphyxiation, and said "Yes. Yes, I want it, I want the job," in a faint, scratchy voice, broken by gasps for air amidst the coughs.

Mitch smiled and laughed. "Alright. Good. There's a beer in that fridge with your name on it. To celebrate. And to, uh, help with the choking."

Striding to the fridge, I snatched the beer, adorned with a red bow, from in front of a shelf full of bags of shredded mozzarella. The first cool, carbonated swig soothed my throat as I walked back over to Mitch.

"As manager, I would like to have a chat about this name," I said, grabbing a pair of food prep gloves out of the dispenser on the gleaming white counter and slipping them over my fingers.

"What—what's wrong with Pizza Pie Palace?" he asked.

"It's quite a mouthful, and sounds like a cheesy kids' place," I explained. "You still have a full bar, so we want it to be somewhere adults feel comfortable coming and hanging out for multiple drinks with their food—hey! you should think about getting a few flat screens for sports."

"I like Pizza Pie Palace," Mitch pouted facetiously.

"You named your titty bar after a swanky suburb of Houston and everyone thought it was a candy store for the first year of operation, Mitch," I chuckled, helping him distribute pepperoni slices over a large crust. "I don't know if you are the best at naming businesses."

"Alright, what do you think it should be called?" he asked. He sprinkled cheese over his work in progress, and the shelf full of shredded cheese flashed in my mind.

"Mozzarella Mitch's," I suggested.

He mulled it over silently for a few moments, then grinned and nodded. "After me? Really?"

"Yeah, people like that," I said. "They see your name, they see you in the kitchen or at the bar or whatever, and they feel like a regular—like a friend you invited. There's a connection and they'll be more likely to come back."

"Hey, you're right, because my favorite donut place is Diane's Donuts, and I always feel like I'm hurting Diane's feelings when I have to go to Dunkin' Donuts instead."

"Yeah, something like that."

"Mozzarella Mitch's," he repeated. "Okay, I like it. I'll get some new shirts made up with a new logo."

"Black," I said. "Black tank tops for the girls and they should all wear denim shorts and white high-top sneakers. Black t-shirts for kitchen and bar staff. And when you're not behind the counter, I want you in black slacks and a white button up shirt with the top two buttons undone."

"Geez, Mick, you got this all figured out, huh?" he chuckled, shooting me an impressed look before taking his pizza to the wood-fire oven.

"Just enjoy colors, and playing dress-up, I guess," I said with a laugh.

The bell on the front door jingled and a group of ten meandered in, checking the place out with curious, wandering eyes. One of them spoke up when the hostess approached. "We saw an ad for a Grand Opening lunch special?"

"You've come to the right place!" Mitch yelled at them with a wave and a smile.

I rushed around the corner and over to greet them with my most charming smile and voice. "Hello! Welcome to Mozzarella Mitch's."

CHAPTER 4

THE CARDINAL SIN

"Mickey!" Mitch yelled from the front door when he arrived.
"Mickey! It's here—it's in today's issue! Mickey! Where are you?"

Popping up from behind the bar like a meerkat from an
underground den, I answered him. "Here! Doing liquor inventory. What's
here? What are you all worked up about?"

He rushed to the bar and slapped a newspaper down on the bar top between us.

"The review!" I squealed and snatched the paper up.

"The review," he echoed with a pleased grin.

"In three short months, Mozzarella Mitch's has not only established itself as the best *new* pizza joint in St. Louis, but maybe the best place to grab a brew and a slice in the city *period*," I read aloud from the review we had been eagerly awaiting for two weeks. My jaw dropped. "Oh my...this is...this is incredible!"

"Keep going," Mitch said with a smile.

"The origins of this Gateway City gem are both hysterical and mystical, slightly unbelievable but certainly not lacking in charm. Formerly a gentleman's club called SugarLand—which sounds like an early, rejected version of a children's board game or a horror film about creatures in the cane plantations of Southern Texas—and owner Mitchell Selkin claims he made the transition from poles to pies in four days after receiving an inheritance from a relative he'd never met. Despite his insistence he had only made one pizza in his life before opening his doors to the public, Mitch makes a mean slice, and he and his fun and funky staff have created several flavor combinations in their three months in the kitchen that will make your head spin and your mouth water.

"When you visit, sit at the bar and chat with the smart and witty manager, Michaela Martin, and try her signature pizza, 'The Cardinal Sin'—a wacky marriage of pineapple (the 'sin'), steak, Dynamite sauce, roasted red pepper, and onion rings that tastes a thousand times better than it sounds. I would say hurry, but I'm confident Mozzarella Mitch's will become a St. Louis institution and be operating for years to come. Four and a half out of five stars."

Mouth gaping again, I locked eyes with Mitch over the top of the paper, his twinkling with delight and mine wild with surprise.

"Champagne?" he suggested with a chuckle.

"Champagne!" I sputtered, fumbling to grab a bottle of Freixenet from the bar fridge. "Yes! A toast!"

He took the bottle from me and popped the cork while I grabbed glasses and set them between us. The gold-tinted liquid fizzed happily as he poured it into the flutes on the bar.

"This is all you," he murmured as we clinked our glasses in a toast.

My cheeks went hot. "No it's not, Mitch," I argued.

"It is! Do you know how many times I get compliments on how nice I look? How often people tell me how great it is to have a pizza place that's not just for kids and families? How great it is to be able to watch the big game while having a gourmet pizza? Those were all your ideas. And you trained the girls, you came up with the names on the menu—Jesus, Michaela, you're so damn creative, on top of being a smoke show. Look at this—look at this dress you're wearing!"

"Stop, Mitch, I'm blushing," I giggled, smoothing the front of the long-sleeved, body-hugging black dress he wildly gestured toward.

"Well, my brother is going to eat you with a spoon," he added casually.

"Your *brother*?!" I choked, nearly spitting out my mouthful of champagne. "I told you, Mitch, I don't want to date right now—I certainly don't want to be set up with your *brother*. We have a great work relationship now, and I don't want to screw that up—"

"Calm down, Martin!" Mitch laughed, holding his hands out in front of him to signal I should stop. "He drove in from Liberty, he's staying with me this week—we're going to the Cardinals game tomorrow. He's just coming for dinner. I am not setting you up."

"You said, verbatim, 'you should date my brother' a month ago, Mitch," I pointed out.

"Yes, I did, but that does not mean tonight is a date. He just wants to try the food and see my place!" he rebutted, his tone casual.

"Wait...has he visited you before? To 'see your place'?" I questioned, a nervous knot in my stomach.

"No," Mitch chuckled and shook his head. "He's a bit too high-brow for that. So don't worry, Martin, he hasn't seen your tits."

"High-brow," I repeated with a scrunch of my face. "What, is he a snob or something?"

"Why do you care? You're not going to date him, right?" he teased.

I rolled my eyes and polished off my celebratory champagne.

"Anyway, he's not a snob, he's just...well, he'll be here for dinner. You'll see."

We were notably busy that day, with not a moment to rest from lunch straight through to dinner. It was the article, the rave review. Mozzarella Mitch's was the place to be. The bar had been especially slammed all day, with everyone ordering my signature pizza and wanting to chat with me. I had been moving nonstop for hours, making drinks and running food, helping the hostess and cleaning tables, but I froze like a statue when Mitch introduced me to his brother—the single most gorgeous man I'd ever laid eyes on.

"Mickey, this is my kid brother, Rafe," Mitch said. "Rafe, my genius first-mate, Mickey Martin."

Rafe extended his hand to me, and I managed to will the correct muscles to do the same.

"A pleasure," Rafe grinned, revealing perfectly straight, sparkling white teeth. His handshake was firm and polite, and ended with a lingering squeeze that sent goosebumps up my arm. Quite abruptly, my normally slumberous libido reminded me I hadn't had sex in over six months, then hinted to me with a rush of hot blood to various regions that it would like to rectify that with the man who stood in front of me.

"Have a seat!" Mitch urged. "You too, Mickey, you've been going like the Energizer Bunny all day. I called in Jenny to help on the bar since we've been so slammed today. She's in back putting her stuff away, so you can take it easy. You guys want a pie?"

Rafe gestured to the polished wood, bar-height chair nearest me and smiled. "Sure, that sounds great, Mitchell," he said once I sat down. He placed a gentle hand on my back as he situated himself in the seat next to me, then took it away to grab the menu Mitch was offering him, but the feel of his palm against my skin remained in the form of a warm tingle.

What the fuck?! I screamed at myself as my eyes roamed over the thin shirt, the aesthetic but not bulging muscles of his upper body, then the perfectly creased and tailored charcoal gray slacks, then the Gucci belt, then below the Gucci belt...

"These names are hysterical," Rafe chuckled as he perused the menu, and even his laugh turned me on.

"That was all Mickey," Mitch said with a grin.

"This one, the, uh, 'Gluten for Punishment'," Rafe laughed. "Perfect. Mitch obviously came up with the recipe, though, right?"

"Yes, that one was me," Mitch admitted.

"You've been putting croutons on your pizza since we were kids," Rafe said with a guffaw. Then he leaned in toward me and nudged my elbow with his, and I tried not to let the fact that the simple and commonplace gesture had turned me into a horny teenager show on my face. "You should have seen the looks our friends would give him when he'd pluck the croutons off the salad and plop them on his pizza," he said to me, but with a teasing grin at his older brother who was pouring three glasses of wine.

"Ha *ha*. Come to town and slander me to my coworkers," Mitch rebutted with a smirk. "I'll have you know that everyone loves the crouton pizza."

"Probably because it has sriracha on it," I muttered.

Rafe placed a hand on my shoulder and laughed out loud, and I could have jumped him right there in that moment, with everyone watching. *Fuck 'em,* I thought, *I don't care—I just need this man's tongue in my mouth right now!*

"Let's have that one. I am a sucker for sriracha," he said to me. My eyes meandered across the features of his face, finally settling on his delectably curved, firm lips, and my stomach churned as I imagined them on the skin of my neck...

"Yeah—yes, of course," I stammered. "Whatever you want to try. They're all great."

"Well, I guess I'll have to keep visiting my brother until I've tried them all," he murmured. We locked eyes and an electric current ran through every inch of my body.

"I guess so," I said in the most alluring voice I could manage in my flustered state.

We talked for hours, laughing and drinking until we were the last two at the bar. I had counted half a dozen instances of casual body contact in that time—'accidentally' bumping knees under the bar and patting my back or grabbing my arm when he laughed at my jokes.

I had lost all track of time, but knew it must be near midnight when Mitch emerged from his office and turned off the televisions, then grabbed himself a beer. "What a day," he groaned in exhaustion.

"You still up for the Cards game tomorrow?" Rafe asked.

"Y'know," Mitch said, shooting me a brief glance, "I think you should take Mickey. I just went last week, and she hasn't been since last year."

"What—no, Mitch, I can't take your ticket!" I protested. "It's your time to spend with your brother."

"I insist," Mitch said. "You deserve a day off. You haven't stopped busting your ass for this place for the last three months."

"I would love it if you came with me, Mickey," Rafe said, and his voice immediately melted my resolve.

"Sure...alright," I agreed. "Okay."

"Great!" Mitch said, slapping the bar triumphantly. "Now, you two get out of here! Kyle needs to mop. Rafe, I'll be home in about an hour. I've gotta run some reports."

"Alright," Rafe replied as he stood from his chair. He reached out for my hand to help me out of my chair, and continued to hold it as we walked across the empty restaurant to the door. Just before we exited, I looked over my shoulder to see Mitch giving me an enthusiastic thumbs up and a comical wink.

Not setting me up, my ass, I thought to myself.

"I shouldn't drive," I grumbled as we approached my car in the lot. "I think we polished off nearly two bottles tonight."

"I'll get us an Uber," Rafe said, pulling out his cell phone and tapping at it to open the app. "I just need to know the destination," he said, a suggestive undertone to his words as he looked up at me from his phone screen.

I couldn't speak—I couldn't even breathe—as our eyes met and exchanged an undeniable recognition of the desire that had built all night. In a flash, he closed the gap between us and pressed me up against my car, his lips covering mine and his hands exploring my midsection.

"God, I'm sorry," he whispered, pulling away and resting his forehead against mine. "I just—you're so fucking beautiful." A broken breath escaped him and the sound of his arousal lit my chest on fire. "I don't know if I can go without you now that I know you exist."

I laughed and bit my lip. "Are you kidding? Have you looked at yourself? You could have any woman you want."

"Well, I want you," he purred as he brought his lips back to mine. The kiss turned from polite to passionate, and his solid body crushed me into my car while his hands clutched at my dress. He pulled away again, and we both gasped for breath. "Let's get that Uber."

"I like your thinking."

CHAPTER 5

TOO GOOD TO BE TRUE

When I woke up the next morning, I kept my eyes closed, too afraid to roll over and see if Rafe had stayed or bolted. My bed felt different, so I wondered if maybe he had stayed...

The baseball game wasn't until two in the afternoon. If he stayed, we'd have hours together in bed. My heart raced at the thought, and my body immediately ached for an encore, or several, of the previous night's performance. Excited by the prospect, I flipped over to my other side and opened my eyes.

Rafe wasn't there.

And this bed wasn't my bed.

I wasn't in my room...

Where the fuck am I?

I shot straight up and rubbed my eyes, then looked around the room, my heart pounding nervously as I did.

Had I been kidnapped? Was this a nightmare?

"Please be a nightmare," I muttered. "Because this looks like the cabin of a..."

Cruise ship. My eyes darted to the porthole, then to the cheesy watercolor of parrots, then the television that looked like it was manufactured in 1980 mounted on the wall. My heart started to pound like a heavy dance hall bass, echoing in my ears and rattling my ribs as if they were bottles of liquor on bar shelves.

Remembering many an urban legend, I quickly checked my lower back for a fresh incision that might indicate I'd had my kidneys harvested for sale on the black market. Thankfully, that potential scenario was a no, but I noticed that I was fully clothed in jeans and a white tank top.

I walked to the porthole and looked out, expecting to see mostly ocean, or some sort of dock, but instead I saw mostly sand with the occasional foam of incoming waves bubbling up along its edge.

"Great, I get mysteriously transported to a cruise ship and it's not even fucking cruising," I muttered, banging my head against the little circular window.

My phone buzzed in my back pocket and I jumped, grabbing it excitedly—I could call for help!

It was a text from Mitch: *Where are you? Rafe said he woke up and you were gone? We're worried.*

Frantically, I tapped out my reply: *I don't know what happened and I'm freaking out. Call the police, please! I'm not hurt, but I'm on a cruise ship and I don't know how I got here!*

I anxiously awaited Mitch's response as the bouncing ellipses on my screen signaled that he was composing it. A warm wave of relief washed over me as a short vibration accompanied a new gray text bubble on my screen.

Wow. Well, I don't really know what to say, Mickey. Rafe will be pretty upset, and I guess I'll have Jenny cover for you while you're gone. Some notice would have been nice.

"What the hell—I need your help, Mitch!" I shouted at my phone.

Mitch—call the police! I'm on a fucking cruise ship and I don't know how I got here!!

Heat filled my cheeks and veins as a dangerous cocktail of anger and adrenaline filled my body.

Mitch's next reply came much quicker: *Jesus, Martin. We get it. You're on a fucking cruise. One that you told nobody you were going on, by the way...not sure why you're rubbing it in.*

I refrained from throwing my phone against the wall, settling for squeezing it in my hands and screaming with my jaw clenched.

How was he completely missing the part where I told him I didn't want to be on the fucking cruise ship and I didn't know how I got on it to start with?

Preparing to type it out in all caps, my eyes darted up the screen to my messages.

They were not what I had typed at all...

The first one read: *Hey, Mitch, I'm totally fine—don't worry. I'm on a cruise! Woohoo!*

"Woohoo? What the fuck?" I said aloud. "I never say *woohoo*..."

The second message read: *It was a last minute decision. Don't be butt hurt! I just needed a vacation. I'm on a fucking cruise ship, motherfuckers!*

I stared at the messages in horror for a second or two, then decided to partake in an experiment.

I typed *"I have been kidnapped,"* and pressed send and before my eyes, the words transformed and the letters rearranged and scrambled and the message that appeared on the screen read *"I'm on a fucking cruise, bitch."*

"Shit!" I spat, stomping around in a circle, trying to release some of the steam that billowed inside me, but all it did was wind me tighter.

Buzz, buzz went the phone in my hand. I expected it, but I jumped anyway. Mitch was certainly not going to have anything nice to say after that last message.

Seriously, Mickey. Brag about this cruise one more time and you're fired. I'm being nice by not firing you as it is. And I really can't believe you would do this to my brother. He really likes you.

My heart dropped and my stomach tied itself in a knot.

Rafe. Poor Rafe. Perfect, hot, smart, sweet, gorgeous, killer-in-the-sack Rafe now thought that I had sex with him a few hours after meeting him then got up in the wee hours of the morning and ditched him for a cruise without saying anything.

The previous day had been one of the best days of my adult life. Obviously, it was too good to be true...

I couldn't fight the urge anymore, and I hurled my phone at the wall, the resulting thud and clatter to the flat-carpeted floor giving me a shred of satisfaction, but it was fleeting.

A knock sounded at the door and my heart did a gymnastics-worth flip.

Kidnappers, surely. *Now* were they coming to take my kidneys?

"Fuck, fuck, *fuck*," I muttered in a raspy whisper.

"Just open the door, I'm not here for your kidneys," came a female voice, low and smooth, and featuring a Spanish accent.

I ran to the door and yanked it open.

"How did you know I was thinking that? Am I part of some mind reading experiment? Is that was this is?" I demanded.

The woman laughed and shook her head. "No, I just remember thinking the exact same thing when I got here."

I stared at her lips as they curled and pursed slightly when she spoke. They were the prominent feature of her round, tan face, their natural curve and pout accentuated by the lilting, rhythmic chords of her rich, pleasing dialect. My eyes shifted up to hers when she finished speaking, and I immediately felt comfortable in their coffee brown watch.

"Can you tell me what is going on, please?" I asked, heat forming in my throat.

"Unfortunately, no," she replied with a grimace. "It's something we all have to figure out for ourselves."

Sobs built up behind the hot stone barrier in my throat, finally breaking through with a sound that resembled the haw of an injured donkey.

"Oh my god, I'm dead!" I bawled. "That's it, isn't it? I'm dead!! Rafe was a psycho killer and he murdered me in my sleep—I knew he was too good to be true! I knew it! Oh my god...just when my life was getting better I had to go sleep with a psycho killer I just met! Why am I so stupid?!" I wasn't even sure if my words were intelligible to the woman as they spewed forth accompanied by wailing sobs. I crumpled against the door frame and slid down it, resting in a heap on the floor.

The woman knelt next to me and swiped away a single tear with her finger. "It's always when your life gets better," she murmured.

Then she stood and walked away. "Lunch is at noon sharp," she added over her shoulder.

Lunch?! I thought. "What the fuck do I need lunch for? I'm dead!" I cried.

A muffled voice boomed from behind another door in the hall. "Shut up! You're not dead! Can you *please* fuck off—some of us have hangovers and it's only nine a.m.!"

With punctuated, labored gasps, I tried to steady my bawling and regain my breath, sliding back into my room and shutting the door.

How many people are on this boat? I wondered as I vigorously wiped the moisture from my cheeks and jaw. *And if I'm not dead...then what the fuck is going on?*

After lying in bed in a state of shock for almost two hours, I finally worked up the nerve to leave the cabin and wander the cruise ship. It was ugly, and old, I noted as I searched for some kind of clue as to what the hell was going on, and tried to figure out how many people were on the damn thing. Making my way toward the dining hall, hoping to find the woman who had checked on me earlier, I jumped when I entered what looked like a showroom lounge and someone called out to me.

"A newbie!"

I whipped around to see the source of the voice—a lanky man with scruffy blond hair standing behind a bar drying glasses.

"Need a drink?" he offered with a smirk.

Something told me this man's face was in a smirk at all times.

"It's eleven in the morning," I stated.

He laughed through his nose and his shoulders bounced. In lieu of a response, he pulled a beer from the tap and slid it toward me on the polished bar top. With a shrug and a sigh, I took the seat in front of the fizzing amber offering.

"I'm guessing you can't tell me what the fuck is going on either?" I asked before I delved into the contents of the glass.

He shook his head. "No...sorry. I could try. It'll be funny."

"What do you mean?" I asked, licking beer foam from my lips and tilting my head.

"Have you called anyone? Or sent a message?" he asked.

"Yes! And the words just change!"

"Well, it's the same if I try to tell you," he explained as he went about getting a glass of beer for himself. "I physically can't. The words will come out as something completely different, and usually pretty weird. Wanna see?"

"Sure," I nodded.

He cleared his throat and tried to wipe the smirk off his face, but a shred of it remained on his wiry lips.

"Hey, is shuffleboard the same as curling, just without ice? Why am I asking you—you're not retired!" he said, his voice sounding completely normal as if he had intended to say exactly that.

I chuckled and took a sip of the refreshing beer at the same time as him.

"That sounds like a bad stand-up joke," I said.

"Well, then I probably had it one of my old sets and this is a cruel irony," he groaned sarcastically.

"Oh, you—you're a comedian?"

"Yes. Todd Drake, and I doubt you've heard of me."

"Why do you say that?"

"Because just as I was about to do a national tour and film a special, I ended up here."

It's always when your life gets better...

The woman's words echoed in my head.

"Things were going pretty well for me, too," I sighed.

"That's how it goes," Todd said with a click of his tongue. "That's the name of the game."

"So I've been told," I muttered.

"So, what was your life like yesterday, uhm..."

"Mickey."

"Mickey," he repeated. "Cute. Tell me what was good, Mickey."

"Well, things had been going great for months, actually," I explained. "I'm the manager at a new pizza restaurant and we just got an amazing review in the paper yesterday."

"Congrats," Todd said, raising his beer for a toast.

"Thanks," I said, clinking my glass against his then taking a drink. "Then last night, I met my boss's brother and he's gorgeous and smart and totally into me for some reason..." I shrugged and trailed off, staring into the bubbling, swirling liquid gold in the glass.

"For some reason?" Todd laughed. "You're kidding, right?"

My head snapped up to look at him. The smirk I'd already grown used to after a few minutes of conversation was prominent on his thin face, and the only other feature that potentially pulled focus from it were his incisive and puckish blue eyes.

"You're not flirting with me already, are you?" I grinned demurely.

"How long did it take dream boy?" he teased, cocking his head at me and taking a casual tug of his booze.

I laughed. "About ten minutes."

"Well, there you have it," Todd smiled. "Continue." He made a swooping, exaggerated gesture of his hand to invite me to proceed.

"Anyway, we were supposed to go to the Cardinals game this afternoon," I muttered. "And now he thinks I ditched him to go on a cruise after one night together. Like, if that's not a one-night stand horror story, I don't know what is."

"It's better this way, Mickey," Todd said. "I mean, better that it was just one night instead of full blown relationship. It would have hurt both of you even more that way."

For once, there was no smirk on his face, and his impish eyes had filled with sympathy.

"Oh god, why are you looking at me like that? I'm never getting out of here, am I?!" I uttered, burying my head in my hands.

"Hey, hey, hey..." he murmured, grabbing my hands and prying them away from my face so he could look me in the eye. "We don't know that. I mean, it's not looking good but—"

I ripped my hands away. "Oh, don't joke about it, please," I barked at him when his lips curled back into their default grin. "Fuck! What did I do to deserve this?!"

Todd raised his eyebrows at me and crossed his arms in front of chest. "Well, that's the question, isn't it?" he said, his tone mischievous. "What *did* you do?"

My stomach churned nervously and my entire body slumped in a heavy defeat.

"How...how long have you—"

"Half a year," he answered before I finished my question. "Two hundred days coming up in a week or two, I believe. I don't know, I guess there's going to be a party." He shrugged his shoulders, then his brows.

"I mean, aren't people looking for you? Jeez, how many people are on this thing?" I asked, panic creeping into my voice. "How long have *they* been here?"

"Oh, I think eleven with you now, and some of them have been here for close to two years," he answered with complete nonchalance.

"This is *insane*! Shouldn't there be people looking for all eleven of us? Police? Detectives? Family members? Friends?"

"No, Mickey, there's not. We told them all we were on a cruise. Like this: *I'm on a cruise, bitches!* Or, oh, when I called the Los Angeles Police Department, I said 'Don't come looking for me, I'm docking in Cancun, motherfuckas!' when I was trying to say 'Please come find me right now, I'm about to piss my pants'."

"*I'm on a cruise, bitch* seems to be popular," I groaned.

He threw his head back and laughed out loud, the crisp, lively ring of it pulling me an inch or two out of my dark and fuzzy haze of self-pity.

"Who did you say that to?" he asked, still slightly chuckling.

"My boss," I grumbled my response. "God, I'm sure he hates me. I'm sure his brother hates me. And if they don't, they will after I've been gone for six months and all I can say to them is 'I'm on a motherfucking cruise, woohoo!' Woohoo, indeed."

I hadn't even realized that I'd finished my beer until Todd pulled my suds-filmed empty glass away and went to rinse it out, his eyes scanning me carefully as he did.

"Still hung up on Dream Boy, hm?" he asked.

"Are you sure you weren't a bartender before this, too?" I asked.

"I was," he smiled. "I wasn't a very good comedian and had to pay the bills. Now, don't avoid the bartender's questions. This is the only therapy you're gonna get on this ship."

"You don't understand, Todd," I sighed. "Guys like Rafe don't come into my life, ever. And they certainly never show interest."

"What kinds of guys do come into your life?" he asked, pulling me another beer from the tap.

"Frat boys who want to know if I have a thigh gap."

He chuckled and slid me the freshly filled glass. "Well, I can help you forget all of them—the perfect one and all the bad ones before him." He leaned over the bar toward me, a hint of flirtation in his confident, comical smirk.

"Mister Drake, are you always this forward?" I asked, placing a hand to my chest in mock appall.

"I'm not sure what you're insinuating, madame," he joked. "I meant with *this*." He slid the beer toward me another inch, sending a cascade of foamy fluid sloshing over the brim and down the side of the glass.

"Oh, of *course*," I drawled, my tone rich with sarcasm.

I found myself scanning him up and down over my glass as I chugged its contents. Outlines of lean muscles were visible through his black t-shirt and his long legs filled out his fitted jeans. I could easily picture him up on a stage, in a spotlight, wearing a stylish leather jacket, his hair spiked with precision and gel. As I moved my eyes back up to his distinct yet youthful and lively face, I realized his eyes roamed over my

features, as well. He grinned and cleared his throat.

"It's almost lunch time," he announced. "Time to meet the rest of

the crew."

CHAPTER 6

PORN AND BOOZE

Oddly nervous at the prospect of meeting a pack of strangers,

even though that was what I had done everyday at Mozzarella Mitch's and

SugarLand for over two years, I followed Todd to the dining room nearby.

The worn carpet was a shade of puce I hadn't seen used in interior design

other than in movies made in the seventies. There were several small

tables covered in dingy pink tablecloths, but the people who had already arrived were gathering around a long table made up of eight square tables pushed together.

A couple in colorful Hawaiian shirts sat at the table already with large sodas and full trays of food, tucking burgundy napkins into their shirts—another thing I had never seen outside of old movies—and a group of three gentleman, all of whom had long whiskers on their chins, two of them looking almost identical, approached their seats but stopped and stared when they saw me trailing Todd into the room.

"Look what we have here," the oldest looking man muttered. "Todd, I hope you're being nice to our new arrival."

"Of course I am," Todd said in a voice that was simultaneously suave and playful. "Nice is my middle name, Herb."

The white-whiskered, disheveled looking man, apparently named Herb, laughed out loud until he began to cough and wheeze as he took a seat next to the man in the touristy get up.

"Your middle name is Arbor because your parents are hippies," Herb fired back once his coughing was under control.

"I think it's beautiful," a middle-aged blonde woman announced with a wink and smile at Todd as she slinked into a seat at the far end of the long table.

"Thanks, Didi," Todd muttered in apparent embarrassment. "Everyone, this is Mickey."

"Hi, Mickey," came various voices, some muffled by mouthfuls of food.

I scanned the table for the woman who had come to my cabin earlier, but she was nowhere in sight.

"Does she know yet?" Herb asked.

"No," Todd replied. "Why don't you all tell her how long it took you to find out why you were here while I go get her a plate."

"No, Todd," I objected, turning to face him, "I can get my own plate, please. I appreciate it, but I don't need special treatment."

"Of course," he grinned. "Well, the buffet's right back here." He placed a gentle hand between my shoulder blades and guided me toward the back of the dining hall where a buffet table sat near the opening into the salmon-tiled kitchen.

"Could they have picked *one* awful shade of pink or purple...?" I muttered under my breath.

Todd let out a raspy laugh next to me. "Maybe you can redecorate," he suggested with a shrug. "I bet you it changes back, though."

"Changes *back*—what? How is that even possible?" I questioned, my face crinkling up in confusion as I whipped my entire body toward him.

His face went tight and filled with pity again. "I-I'm sorry, I can't explain it—"

"Right," I snapped, "of course. Nobody can tell me what the fuck is going on. I have to figure it out for myself."

"Once you remember, everything will make sense, I promise."

"Remember *what*?" I growled in frustration, throwing my hands in the air.

"I know this is scary," he said, placing his hands on my shoulders to comfort me, "but you *will* figure it out, and it *will* get easier."

His thumbs ran over my skin and, in my annoyed, fuming state, I pulled away from him—bumping right into someone behind me. They let out a soft whimper of surprise and I spun around quickly, ready to apologize, but had to look down a foot to do so. I had bumped into a kid, a kid with jet black hair and a plate full of tacos.

"Hey, Lucian," Todd greeted him. "This is Mickey."

The boy looked me up and down and then went back to piling food on his plate.

"I'm sorry I bumped into you," I said. He looked at me again for a moment, then went right back to ignoring me.

"He's shy. He's the only kid here," Todd said. "Lucian, I'm guessing the kitchen is a mess and she won't come out until it's spotless?"

Lucian nodded as he plopped a hefty serving of flan next to his tacos and headed toward the table without a word.

Todd plucked a piece of seasoned chicken out of its chafing dish and tossed it into his mouth. "Alright, I'm gonna go help in the kitchen. Here's the food, kid." He winked and started to walk into the kitchen on his own.

I looked at the food, then back to the long table of people who were sure to interrogate me if I went and sat with them. The decision to follow Todd came as suddenly and spontaneously as the necessary muscular movements to rush after him.

"Can't stay away, hm?" he teased when I caught up with him as he approached a large tiled island, strewn with dishes and mess. "Cat! Come eat, everyone is going to finish without you."

"You know that's how I prefer it!" came a familiar voice from the dish station at the back of the kitchen. The accent, the rich depth, the lilting cadence...

The woman from that morning rounded the dish steamer column and made her way toward the island, drying her hands on a red apron and eying me intently as she did.

"Ah, you have a puppy today, do you, Drake?" she remarked.

"Mickey, this is Cat," Todd said, gesturing between us. "Cat, Mickey."

"We've met," she said nonchalantly, pulling her shoulder length black-brown hair into a ponytail and securing it with a band from around her wrist. "And I'm *Catalina*, not 'Cat'. Todd shortens everyone's names—as he's already done for you, it seems."

"Nope, that's what she told me," Todd rebutted with a shrug. "Mickey."

"Mickey?" Catalina chuckled icily as she stacked mixing bowls from the island. "That is a name for a cartoon mouse, not a lady."

"Well, maybe I'm not a lady," I muttered.

Catalina's eyes darted up to meet mine and Todd chortled next to me.

"See, Cat? Not everyone dislikes nicknames," Todd continued in glee.

"Herb does," Catalina stated coolly, turning her gaze from me to Todd.

"Well, tough shit for Herb," Todd laughed. "I'm not saying the name Herbert to a man who is here because of porn and booze."

My head snapped to him. "What?"

"If he tries to explain it further it will come out as one of his awful stand-up jokes," Catalina groaned.

"Alright, I think I'm gonna go eat, actually," Todd said with a forced grin, then he tapped his fingers on the tile of the island. "Have fun with your dishes, Catalina."

He turned and made his way out of the kitchen, and I could feel her eyes on me as, once again, I followed him. When we reached the buffet and assembled our plates, I muttered under my breath to him: "What is her deal? She seemed nice to me this morning."

"She can be very caring—maternal instinct, I guess—but for the most part, she's like that," he explained.

"Maternal instinct," I echoed. "Wait a minute—*Lucian*?!"

Todd nodded. "And she carries a lot of guilt over the fact that he's here, and he didn't do anything."

"How long have they been here?"

"Just over a year. The day before Lucian was supposed to be going into fourth grade at a private school for science and math—she's pretty torn up about it, and she blames herself. And it makes her more cold and distant every passing day."

My face pulled into a frown as I imagined how she felt. I didn't even know what was going on yet but I knew I'd feel terrible if I pulled an innocent person into it with me, especially it were my *child*.

"Look, don't worry about her too much," Todd intervened. "From the sounds of it, she was a pretty hardened *mujer* when she got here. She's had it rough, but she can handle it."

"You speak Spanish?" I asked, cocking my head.

"Uh, not her Spanish," he answered, jerking his head toward the kitchen to indicate Catalina. "She's from Argentina. But, I've lived in L. A. my whole life. I took it in school. I've even done a few stand up shows in Spanish."

"Impressive," I remarked.

"Oh yeah, it was the most engaged audience I've ever had," he chuckled. "I mean, they were mostly engaged in calling me a 'skinny white asshole' and shouting about my tiny dick in Spanish, but they laughed a lot, which is what I wanted, right?"

"Oh," I uttered awkwardly.

"Don't worry," he joked as we walked back to the table with our trays, "I showed them that I *don't* have a tiny dick and I never got rehired at that bar again."

"You're not serious," I gasped, my lips twisting with amusement and my eyes going wide.

"I am completely serious," he said. "I, uh, was under the influence...of some things."

Again, I felt awkward, and I was quiet until we took seats next to each other at the long table where it appeared that most everyone had finished eating, except Didi, who picked at a large taco salad and jabbered at the rest of them about the activity schedule.

"Toddy, when do you think we should have another luau by the pool?" Didi asked, leaning over the table in his general direction which pushed her bursting bosom up toward her chin. "The last one was so much fun, Mickey! You'll see."

"You all know how much work that was for Catalina," Todd said. "She roasted an entire pig for it—and she had to catch the pig first. So, why don't you ask her when she's ready to do it again?"

"Because she's a bitch," Didi said.

"Didi!" Todd admonished.

"What, Toddy?" Didi purred innocently, a hand to her ample cleavage. "She may have you all fooled with her poor tragic past bologna, but where I come from, a woman like that is called a bitch." She paused briefly to laugh at herself. "Actually, she'd be called 'the maid'—"

"Didi!" Todd barked, this time much louder. "I swear to god, shut your mouth if you're going to be like that."

"Like what, Toddy?" she taunted, running a finger across a gaudy gold necklace that laid perfectly atop her protruding chest.

"Like a racist upper-class white asshole," Todd said, staring her down without the slightest indication he thought her behavior was as cute as she thought it was.

A momentary flash of dejection showed on her face, but it didn't last long before she adopted a facetious, flirty pout. "Well, if we don't do a luau, what should our party for your two-hundredth day be?"

"I don't know, Didi," he sighed. "I don't really want one, and if you insist on throwing one, activity planning is your job, not mine."

"What do you mean, *job*?" I asked.

"Everyone has a job," Herb explained. "We choose based on what we're good at, or have experience in from...before."

"Tracie ran a housekeeping company," Todd said, gesturing to the woman in the Hawaiian shirt, "so she does the housekeeping. Her husband, Bob, was a maintenance man for a huge bank, so he does any maintenance we need. I was a bartender, so I'm the bartender."

"I'm the pool boy," Herb announced, his voice thick with irony, and I laughed along with the rest of the table.

Didi interrupted the conversation with an emphatic slap of her hand on the table to signal she'd had an idea. "I've got it! A burlesque night!"

"Isn't that like striptease?" Tracie asked.

I inhaled sharply and choked on my bite of chicken taco. Todd turned to me and patted me on the back, and Didi's eyes narrowed on me like she were a hawk and I were a mouse in tall grass.

"Are you okay?" Todd asked.

"Yes," I coughed. "I'm fine."

"Yes, Tracie. Burlesque does feature a little female striptease," Didi answered Tracie but never took her eyes off of me, and a wicked smile curled her ruby-glossed lips. "I am sure we can find someone with experience."

Grabbing the nearest glass of water, I guzzled it down, my heart racing and palms sweaty.

"I don't want to see you strip, Didi," Todd said. "How about no burlesque night? I don't think I want anyone to do a striptease for me."

"Suit yourself," Didi sneered.

"So, Mickey, what did you do before...before today?" Tracie asked,

76   Jessica Benoist-Young

her voice timid and clearly just trying to change the topic Didi had started.

My voice raspy from the choking flt, I cleared my throat and answered. "I was the manager at a pizza restaurant."

"Like a Pizza Hut?" Bob asked.

"No, it was more of a sit-down place," I explained. "We had a bar, and TVs to watch sports, and a full wait staff."

"Yesterday, they got a very good review from a food critic for the paper," Todd said.

"Oh! Congratulations!" Tracie cooed with delight, then seemed to remember our collective circumstances and her face dropped.

"Thank you," I muttered.

"Hey!" Herb elated. "Maybe you can help Catalina in the kitchen as your job. She's been struggling since we climbed into double digits."

"Oh, don't do that to her," Didi said, waving a dismissive hand at the idea. "She seems like a sweet girl. The Argentine Terror would break her. Is there something else you're good at sweetie?" Didi tilted her head at me and batted her long, black lashes.

"Uhm, no—well, yes," I stammered nervously. "I—my college degree is in photography."

"Well, I am sure that will come in handy," Tracie said enthusiastically, though I couldn't imagine when or why it would. Her husband shot her a bewildered look that suggested he was thinking the same thing I was.

"Not really a full-time skill, though," Herb stated. "I'm tellin' you, the kitchen."

"Cat does need help," Todd said, giving me a look of strained contemplation. "But I don't want to force you to do anything you don't want to do."

"No, no," I said. "I'll do it. Sure. I mean, if she needs help, that's what I'll do. I'm not a five-star chef or anything."

"And these aren't five-star ingredients, honey," Didi drawled, disgust dripping from her tone and expression.

"Alright, well...I'll tell her you'll start in the morning then," Todd said with a warm smile. My eyes flickered to the glint of his faultless, pearly teeth in the bright fluorescent light.

"Great!" Didi uttered in satisfaction. "*Now* can we have a luau?!"

CHAPTER 7

LITERALLY

After dinner, everyone made their way to the bar, where games of darts and cards and an hour or so of half-hearted karaoke helped pass the time. Everyone but Catalina and Lucian, that is. Didi continued to shoot me knowing glances and warning glares, and practically groped Todd in front of the whole group when the two sang a duet, running her manicured hands up and down his torso, and then "accidentally" too far down more than once.

Throughout the evening, I met everyone I hadn't already been introduced to at lunch. Besides Herb, the other two men with beards were Jeff and Jeric, twin brothers from Alaska who were deep-sea fishermen before arriving on the cruise ship. They were younger than Herb by over a decade, but their scraggly, white-streaked orange whiskers and weathered skin made them appear older than their forty years. There was also Vivienne, a striking black woman in her sixties from France. She knew very little English, just enough to introduce herself, and she left the post-dinner festivities after one glass of meticulously selected red wine.

Jeff and Jeric knew a lot about sailing, even thought the cruise wasn't doing that at the moment, and survival. They had tried fishing many times, in hopes of supplementing the food stocks on the ship, but they told me everything they caught would disappear when they brought it on board.

"Disappear?" I laughed with my bottom lip poised on the rim of a beer-filled pint glass. "How is that possible?"

They looked at each other and shrugged. Then said in unison: "It just disappears."

According to Todd, Vivienne, whenever asked about her life before the cruise ship or what jobs she might be able to help out with, always said one word: "*Retraite*."

"It means 'retired'," Didi enlightened, haughty in her knowledge of one French word. "Anyway, she's fabulous at choosing wine and music, so she helps me with parties when she feels like it. Oh, just you wait until Toddy's party!"

"Right..." I groaned. A party with a bunch of strangers on a creepy, fucked up, decrepit, beached cruise ship that I still had no idea how I came to be on. "The anticipation is killing me."

Knowing I would need to be up early to help in the kitchen, and already three pints down, I quietly slipped out of the lounge around midnight while the entire rest of the group started a raucous karaoke rendition of a song that was vaguely familiar to me but I couldn't recall the name of as I wandered through the halls, letting the few lyrics I knew tumble around in my head.

"Pleased to meet you..." I sang almost inaudibly as I reached the hall where I was mostly positive my room was located. "Hope you guess my name."

It was the Rolling Stones—I could hear the words in Mick Jagger's voice in my head.

"But what's puzzlin' you is the nature of my game..."

My heart flipped when I finished murmuring the lyric. I crashed against the door to my room as I tried desperately to remember the lyrics and the name of the song.

"Pleased to meet you, hope you guess my name...but what's confusin' you is the nature of my game..."

"Just as every cop is a criminal," came a familiar voice down the hall. I jumped and spun toward it, but I knew who it was.

Catalina poked her head out of a room three doors down, exhaustion smeared across her face, but her wide eyes rich with understanding.

"And all you sinners saints," I sang.

She slipped out into the hallway completely, and she wore men's boxers and a lacy camisole, a sleepwear combination that I normally would have gotten a chuckle out of if I weren't racking my brain for not only the lyrics, but why they were prickling the lobes of my brain.

"As heads is tails," Catalina continued to sing, walking slowly toward me in the hall, "just call me—"

"Lucifer..." I uttered in a shocked, breathless whisper.

We stared at each other in silence for several moments while the word hung over my head like a swarm of bees.

"Sympathy for the Devil," I said, remembering the name of the song.

She nodded, and a flash of a grin curled her lips for a brief moment, but her eyes still surveyed me carefully.

Thumping footsteps sounded out and reverberated through the hallway as Todd jogged down it, rushing past Catalina without acknowledging her and stopping in front of me, slightly winded.

"You left, without saying anything," he panted. "I figured you were going to bed, but I just wanted to check. Anyway, you left right in time. Didi just suggested strip poker, so I'm not going back up there."

Strip poker. I fell back against the door as pieces of the puzzle hit me all at the same time. Todd shuffled toward me and grabbed my shoulders, his face contorted with worry.

"Are you okay?" he uttered.

"She's fine," Catalina declared. "She's putting it together."

Todd's face lit up and he pulled me away from the door, then opened it behind me and guided me into my room, positioning me on the bed. Catalina followed him and stood a few feet behind, both of them eying me with anticipation and concern. Kneeling in front of me, Todd placed a hand on my knee.

"Close your eyes," he murmured.

The words triggered a memory, the one that had been trying to break through. It was recent but it was strangely buried in my mind—not by any conscious effort of my own...

I shut my eyes tight and relived the scene, a faint of echo of my own voice saying '*close your eyes*'. I had pulled that shitty fraternity kid into the backroom of the strip club and circled him like a predator, toying with prey, and then I had stripped him down.

An alarm blared in my head and lights flashed, and Mitch was yelling.

What did you do, Martin?

What is your problem?

What did I tell him? *I hated my job. I hated stripping. I would have given anything to never do it again. No, not just anything....*

My eyes popped open and both Todd and Catalina stared at me eagerly.

"No..." I groaned, shaking my head. "No, I—that's not...that can't be —"

"It is," Catalina said.

"Do you remember saying it?" Todd asked.

"Yes, but I didn't mean it *literally*!" I cried in frustration jumping up from the bed, causing Todd to do the same. Then my face dropped and body slumped in defeat. Todd snorted through his nose and his grin took its rightful place upon his lips.

"What?" Catalina snapped. "Why are you laughing?"

"You said '*literally*' when you said it, didn't you?" he teased.

"Yes," I admitted with a frown.

"So did I," he admitted with a crisp guffaw.

"Americans," Catalina sighed and cradled her head in one hand while it shook in disapproval.

I sat back down on the bed and Todd plopped down next to me.

"I...I sold my soul to the Devil," I muttered in shock.

In my peripheral vision, I saw Todd nodding his head. "You did," he confirmed.

"And everything was awesome...for three months!"

"I got five," Todd said.

"I got a year," Catalina added.

"I thought the circumstances of Mitch's sudden desire to close the strip club and open a pizza place were a little fishy, but, I was just so excited and caught up in it, I just didn't care."

They both looked at me in silence and a surge of embarrassment flooded my gut as I realized I had just revealed a new piece of information to them—to two people who were strangers to me when I woke up this morning...

"Yes, I was a stripper," I added dejectedly. "For two years. And I had anger management issues and a really bad night, and took this dumb guy's pants and pulled the fire alarm and that's when I said it. I sold my soul to Satan to never have to strip again."

Todd chuckled next to me. "Why'd you pull the fire alarm?"

"I wanted the lights to come on while he was half naked in the VIP room," I shrugged. "He was a dick."

"Making a note to myself not to get on your bad side," he murmured playfully.

"What about you?" I asked, turning to look at him. "Fame?"

He shrugged his eyebrows and pursed his lips. "Yep. I wish I could say I wanted fame just for success and achievement, but...I really just wanted the money."

I remembered him mentioning his flashing incident, and how he had been under the influence.

"Drugs?" I whispered.

He nodded, his eyes dropping to look in his lap, but didn't say anything.

I looked up at Catalina, who had been silently watching us the whole time. Our eyes locked and I didn't have to verbalize my questions. She knew what information I sought.

"Lucian had a brain tumor," she stated plainly. "Now he doesn't."

"That's good," I said. "Better than a pizza restaurant."

"Better than drugs," Todd chimed in.

"Lucian will live a healthy life now."

"Here?" she let loose an icy laugh.

"Well, it's not like we'll be here forever," I muttered, not even convinced of my own words, as I had absolutely no idea how long we would be stuck on the cruise ship.

"For a child, any amount of time away from a normal life is too much time," she said.

"Well, things are different in Argentina, then," Todd scoffed. "My childhood was nowhere near anything resembling a normal life."

"Mine either," I agreed with Todd.

"And look what happened to you both," she said gesturing to us. "A stripper with anger issues and a drug addicted comedian."

"You know, Cat?" Todd barked. "I always stand up for you and I have really tried my hardest to be amicable—nice and helpful even—but I've had it with your judgy shit." He turned to me. "If you don't want to work with her in the kitchen, I completely understand, Mickey."

I shook my head. "No, it's fine," I said. "It will be fine." I stared her down and she stared back. I had been her before—"not very nice"—it was stand-offish posturing to keep people at a distance, to scare them away. She wanted to be feared, and she wanted to be left alone. I could play that game, too.

Catalina scanned me with narrowed eyes one last time before turning and leaving the room without a word.

"Good luck tomorrow," Todd sighed, patting me on the back. "You should probably get some sleep. You must be drained."

"Todd..."

"Yeah, Mickey?"

"Why a cruise ship?" I asked. "Why does he want us all *here*?"

He stood and shrugged. "Your guess is as good as mine. And my guess is he's just fucking with us."

At dawn, I rolled out of bed, completely naked—which is not how I went to sleep. I jumped up and wrapped the sheet from the bed around me, even though no one else was around. My eyes darted to a suitcase with a red gift-wrap bow on it sitting atop the desk in my cabin. I unzipped it and opened it with caution. Knowing who my host was, I half-expected some sort of psychotic prank, like a suitcase full of snakes, or something to jump out and scare me. Much to my relief, it was just clothes, and I pawed through them looking for something to wear.

There was a trick of some kind in the suitcase, though, I realized as I went through the garments. They were all overtly sexy items of clothing. Skimpy, eye-catching, short and cut where short and cut would have the most impact.

Prurient, I thought with both disdain and mild amusement.

I had never dressed like this in my life. I was a jeans and t-shirt girl, or occasionally a nice, classy, comfortable dress or skirt. Holding each article in front of my face and scrutinizing it, I was strangely happy to

89

finally find a pair of Daisy Duke shorts and a bedazzled, low cut St. Louis Cardinals tank top. All the undergarments in the suitcase were red and lacy pushup bras and thongs.

"Funny," I grumbled at Satan, wherever the fuck he was, as I pulled out one of each. I dropped the sheet and dressed reluctantly in the outfit that was sure to guarantee a lot of stares. *I could just spend the whole day in the kitchen*, I thought as I made my way through the hallway toward my job assignment. But, Catalina probably already thought I was a promiscuous slut, if her statements about how I 'turned out' were any indication. So maybe the kitchen wasn't the best place for me to hide.

Groggy from a night of tossing and turning, I trudged into the kitchen and immediately searched for a source of caffeine. The initial survey of the counter tops revealed none, but out of the corner of my eye, a curl of steam signaled me to the presence of hot liquid. I whipped toward it and saw Catalina cradling a white mug and staring at me over reading glasses in wide-eyed surprise.

"Coffee?" I uttered.

Wordlessly, she pointed to a small office behind me, and I spun on my heels and rushed to the little coffee maker on the desk within.

"Or there's an espresso machine in the bar," she called to me as I grabbed the pot and prepared to pour. I froze, considering my options.

"But I would go now, before Todd gets there, if I were you."

Coffee pot and mug held aloft in each hand, I looked down at my appearance. Red lace didn't just peek out of the white, sparkling tank, it jumped out and begged for attention, demanded that all eyes survey the rolling hills of my chest and the valley of cleavage between them. There was a gap of two inches between the bottom of the shirt and the top of the low-waisted shorts, and featured in that gap were my naval and my pelvic bones. My lean, sinewy legs were showcased in all their bare glory, smooth and shining in the flood of fluorescent lighting.

"I didn't—" I started, but Catalina interrupted.

"I know," she said. "You didn't want to wear it. Here, start the waffle batter and I'll go get you a cappuccino, *si*? You have made waffles before?"

I nodded and handed her the ceramic mug when she approached.

"Perfect. Dry or wet?" she asked.

I cocked my head at her. "The waffles?"

"No," she grinned. "Your cappuccino. How much foam?"

"Oh, dry. A lot of foam. I like to sprinkle raw sugar in it."

She bit her lip and laughed through her nose. "So do I," she murmured. "I wonder what else we have in common."

Feeling the skin of my face and the tops of my ears go warm under the intensity of her brown-eyed gaze, I rambled through an attempt at humor. "I think painting toenails is stupid, I strongly dislike country music, and I believe deep-fried sushi is superior to raw sushi."

"You are wrong about raw fish," she declared. "I will make you my ceviche sometime. The next time I get *decent ingredients*." Her eyes shifted down to the floor and she seemed to speaking directly to someone beside me.

"Oh, he...he actually listens?" I asked awkwardly.

"Listens, watches, interferes," she answered. She gestured to my outfit and raised her eyebrows. "Play and toys and taunts."

"You think...you think we are his..."

"Playthings?" she said. "Personal *telenovela*? That is precisely what I think. And he is wasting no time using you to start drama today," she added, a hint of disdain tinging her pleasant, deep voice. "Anyway, I would refrain from getting to know anyone too well until he decides it's not funny to exploit your...*assets*...for his amusement."

She turned and left the office, and then the kitchen, and I felt oddly unsettled and unnerved. My palms were sweaty when I went to gather the ingredients for the waffle batter. Catalina returned just as I finished combining them all in the mixing bowl, and besides instructing me in which fruit to cut up for fruit salad and where to find the dishes and flatware, she hardly spoke to or looked at me for the rest of the morning.

After breakfast, she left without a word, piles of dirty dishes scattered across the kitchen that apparently I was expected to do. I finally finished sanitizing them all and cleaning the counter tops at ten thirty—only half an hour before we were supposed to start prepping lunch. Storming out of the kitchen, I made beeline for the lounge, not giving one fuck who saw me.

I needed a fucking drink.

CHAPTER 8

ST. LOUIS SLUT BARBIE

"Well, good morning!" Todd beamed at me as I approached the bar. "How was...uh...kitchen duty?" His speech slowed as I got closer and ripped off the apron I had put on during dish duty, and his eyes scanned me up and down, then up and down once more.

I didn't respond, just came around behind the bar in determination.

"Okay..." he drawled. "I guess you can get your own drink."

He stood right in front of the tap, drying a pint glass, I snatched it out of his hand and pushed him out of the way with my shoulder to fill it with beer.

"Hey! St. Louis Slut Barbie!" he barked. "What the fuck is going on?"

"I need a drink!" I snapped, guzzling the foamy beer I pulled from the tap.

"Yeah, I got that much," was his retort. "Hey, slow down—Mickey, did something happen?"

"I don't want to talk about it," I replied crisply after draining the entire glass. "I just want to drink."

"Look, Mickey—" he started, but I cut him off.

"What, Todd?!"

"It's like ten thirty in the morning—"

"Isn't this how you said you were going to help me?" I asked facetiously, setting my beer back on the grate under the tap, preparing to pour another. I gestured to the bar with flailing arms. "This? All of this? To help me forget?!"

"You know that's not actually what I meant," he said awkwardly. "I was obviously hitting on you—you knew that—"

"Well then, help me forget," I uttered in frustration.

"What? What are you talking about?"

"Help me forget!" I repeated, my tone more urgent and somewhat challenging.

He laughed through his nose and shook his head. "No—"

"Why not?! You don't want me?"

"That's not it."

"Then what? Hm? All that flirting yesterday for nothing—"

"Not like this, Mickey, god damnit," he snapped, his face going hard like I had yet to see.

We stared each other down, his pale blue eyes burning into mine as neither of us moved or made a sound besides our breaths. My heart raced, and I couldn't tell if it was solely from anger. I felt strangely unsettled by Catalina's fluctuations between friendly and frigid, but I didn't know why, and on top of the despair of being on the ship in general —this Devil's Cruise—I knew I needed some sort of outlet for my frustrations, whether it be distraction or destruction.

"Fine," I finally said. "I ask you for help and you can't do it, so I'll just help myself."

He sighed. "Mickey, don't be like that."

"Where's the vodka?" I demanded, ignoring him.

"Mickey..."

I spotted a large bottle of Smirnoff in the well right next to him. He saw my eyes flash to it and instinctively moved even closer to the well in an attempt to block me from it.

"Todd, move."

"Mickey, stop."

"Don't tell me what to do," I snapped.

"You're telling me what to do!" he argued.

I tried to shove him to the side, but he was expecting it, his body tensed. He was much stronger than his lean frame suggested. "Just move!"

"I'm not letting you get shitfaced before lunch just so you can cope with whatever the hell is going on in your head!" he declared emphatically.

"You're not *letting me*?" I spat.

"No, I'm not," he said.

"Ha!" I laughed out loud. "You think because I followed you around like a scared little puppy yesterday that you can make decisions for me now? If you don't want me to, why don't you just help me like I asked you to?!"

"Fine!" he barked, grabbing me by the hips and pulling me against him abruptly. I inhaled sharply when we collided together and he dropped his face down toward mine. "Is this what you want?" he asked, his voice a soft murmur.

I nodded, but couldn't speak, my breath coming in short, shallow pants against a fire in my chest.

"Right here?" he whispered, his lips brushing against mine. "In the bar?"

He swung me to the side and pressed my backside into the edge of the bar top and I gasped, clutching at his chest instinctively. My response spurred him on and he grabbed the back of my thigh and pulled my leg up to his side as he sucked my bottom lip in between his teeth. Moving of their own accord, my hands snaked up and around to the nape of his neck and a growl of want rumbled in his chest as his mouth covered mine.

"Ahem."

We jumped and broke our lips apart at the sound of someone clearing their throat behind us, but Todd didn't take his hands away from their positions, one on my bare thigh and the other on the small of my back. He looked over my shoulder to the throat-clearer, a slight ironic smirk on his face and his eyes narrowed in a playful warning glare.

"Bob," he said. "How can I help you?"

"Didi wanted to go over the drink menu for the luau," Bob replied awkwardly.

"Of course she does," Todd sighed. "Where is she?"

"In her room," Bob answered.

"I'm not going to her fucking room," Todd said, his voice and face going serious in a flash. "And you can tell her that, word for word."

I heard Bob shuffle away and out of the lounge, but never took my eyes off Todd's face through the whole exchange. My chest heaved, rising and falling as I tried to steady my breath, a task at which I was not succeeding.

"If she hears about this from Bob, she's going to be insufferable," Todd groaned, his fingertips digging into my thigh and lower back.

"She wants you," I murmured, partially questioning, but mostly stating—I had noticed her behavior toward him the day before.

"She's had me," he admitted with a tinge of disgrace in his voice, and he finally let go of me and stepped away.

"Oh," I muttered.

"This..." he sighed and gestured to my clothes. "This was a *gift,* I'm assuming?"

I nodded, frozen in place against the bar, still feeling his hands on my body even though he had taken them away.

"Was there anything else?" he asked, eying me with suspicion.

"What? No," I answered. "Just a suitcase full of skanky clothing."

"Are you sure?" he pressed in his interrogation

"Yes! I'm sure. Why? What else would there be?" I questioned.

"Nothing," he muttered, his face tight. "Nothing. Never mind. Don't worry about it. You should go get ready for lunch." He stooped down to pick up my apron off the floor and handed it to me. "I will see you later?"

"That depends," I stated, snatching the apron from his offering hand and slipping it over my head.

"On what?" he cocked his head.

"On whether or not Catalina leaves me to do all the cleaning for every meal," I replied as I tied the apron behind my back. "I might be washing dishes and scrubbing the floor until midnight."

"Ah," he sounded knowingly. "Well, you could always leave it. That's what I do."

"I'm sure she'd *love* that," I groaned.

"Why do you care what she thinks, Mickey?" he asked.

I had no answer for him, and an awkward silence fell between us, a thick net of unresolved tension that snared us both in its swath. I turned and strode out of the lounge, not able to handle it anymore. Out of the corner of my eye, just before I exited the room, I saw him go back to his own sink full of the previous night's dishes.

My stomach twisted nervously as I made my way back to the kitchen for round two with the Argentine Terror, and I lamented not grabbing a beer to go...

Lucian sat on the pink-tiled island, swinging his legs and staring at the screen of a hand-held device of some kind as his mother bustled around the kitchen, sighing and clicking her tongue in disapproval.

"What's wrong?" I ventured, immediately regretful I did. I had resolved not to speak with her unless necessary, but as soon as I saw her, dark brows furrowed and pacing anxiously, that resolve all but washed away, like a castle of sand on the beach in high tide.

"Oh," she said, jumping a bit, as if she didn't know I was there until I spoke. "I...well, every day, for every meal, we get fresh ingredients in the refrigerator and that's what I have to cook with."

"You have to cook whatever he wants you to?" I scoffed in disbelief.

"*Si*," she answered with a nod. She bit her lip and stared at me imploringly.

"Well, what is it today?" I asked.

"Nothing," she stated, a pouting frown drawing her full lips downward.

"Oh," I uttered. "Shit."

"Yes," she sighed. "Shit."

She pulled a face, remembering that Lucian sat on the island and had heard her swear.

"Lucian, go play that in the lounge," she ordered, and he hopped down obligingly, trudging out of the kitchen without a single peep.

When he was gone, I sighed and scratched my head. "Okay, well, there are ingredients—like pantry staples—that aren't fresh, right?"

"Sure, a few things, but I don't know what to do with them!" Catalina cried in frustration, her accent thickening in her distress. "I worked my way through college at a five-star restaurant in Buenos Aires! I cook with real food, not your American bullshit in boxes!"

I snorted through my nose and tried not to let my amusement show too much on my face, which led to me tucking in my lips to suppress a grin.

"Oh, this is funny to you?" she snapped.

I shrugged as I walked past her toward the cabinets where I had found the flour for the waffles that morning. "I happen to be an expert at American bullshit in boxes."

Scanning the cupboard, I saw several things I could use: boxes of instant rice, economy sized cans of crushed tomatoes, a few different varieties of beans, and more. I looked behind me to the open shelves under the island, seeing plenty of spices, as well as dried chiles and a basket of onions.

"Alright," I said, pulling out the ingredients I needed for a dish I knew like the back of my hand, "I will make lunch, but you're on dish duty for the rest of the day."

"Fine," she sighed, waving away my request like it were inconsequential. "What are you making?"

"Have you ever had Indian food?" I asked.

"*You* know how to cook Indian cuisine?" she jeered.

"Oh, I'm sorry, did I assume the only thing you know how to make is Spanish food because you're from Argentina?" I teased. "Just because I'm white, I can't cook ethnic cuisine?"

"More like since you're young, I figured you couldn't cook anything that took more than ten minutes and one pot on the stove."

"I did a semester abroad in London, and my flatmate was from India," I explained. "She taught me how to make a few dishes. Are you familiar with *dal*?"

"Yes, the lentil soup," she nodded. "Our place in New York is near an Indian restaurant that serves it with all the entrees, free of charge."

"You live in New York?" I asked, spreading out the ingredients while she gathered pots for the rice and lentils.

"Yes, Manhattan. We moved there from Buenos Aires when Lucian was three," she answered. "I got a job teaching at NYU."

"You're a professor?"

"I am. Biology."

"Wow. So, you're a genius," I laughed.

She didn't respond, but I looked just in time to see her cheeks blush a warm pink, almost matching the tile of the kitchen counters.

"So," I said, changing the subject, "you moved from Buenos Aires with...with Lucian's father?"

"Ha!" she uttered, throwing her head back. "No, no. My girlfriend. Well, ex-girlfriend. She left me when Lucian was diagnosed with his tumor."

"Holy shit," I rasped.

"Yes. Holy shit."

"What a bitch!" I remarked.

Catalina grinned and nodded. "She *was* kind of a bitch. Anyway, good riddance to bad rubbish."

"No kidding," I sighed. "Is there a pressure cooker in here?"

Concentration scrunched the features of her round face, until she appeared to remember its location and rushed off to find it, returning a moment later with it cradled in her arms.

"Perfect," I hummed, dumping the coral-colored lentils inside it and covering them with broth and water, then placing the pressure cooker on the stove top. Catalina put the rice on the burner next to it, accidentally brushing her shoulder against me as she did.

"Sorry," she muttered.

"No problem," I replied, feeling my own cheeks tinge with pink.

We moved back to the island in a clumsy, unintentional unison.

"Should I do a flat bread?" I asked, and she nodded, sliding me a mixing bowl and the tub of flour.

"So," she started, her tone tentative, "what about you?"

"What about me what?" I echoed, not taking my eyes up from measuring the flour.

"Anyone back in...St. Louis?" she questioned.

"No, not really," I sighed.

"Not really...?"

"There was maybe going to be someone, but I'm here now, so I'm guessing it's over," I explained.

She was quiet for a few moments, and I could feel her surveying my face, but I didn't look up at her, feeling strangely self-conscious under her gaze.

"Maybe it's not," she finally said, her voice soft and tone supportive. "Maybe it was meant to be, and it will pick back up. You never know."

I shrugged. "I guess you're right," I muttered. "You never know."

We prepped the lunch together, at first in silence, but then in casual conversation about our favorite parts of New York, and our least favorite ones. I had visited a few times when I was younger and recounted my trips to her in detail, and since many of them were college road trips, she laughed at my escapades in young adult debauchery and how vastly it varied from her mellow, single mother daily routine.

After we took the finished meal to the banquet table, we brought our dishes back to the kitchen and, even though I had exchanged my recipe and guidance for dish duty, I helped her clean up while we grazed on our rations and discussed the famous nineteen-inning Mets versus Cardinals game from 2010.

"I had just moved to New York from Buenos Aires, and was at a party thrown by a colleague," she recounted between bites of flat bread. "His teenage sons had the game on, and somehow we got sucked into staying until it was over."

"It was seven hours!" I laughed. "And you were on the east coast!"

"God, I was exhausted," she giggled, "and I distinctly remember wondering if I had made a huge mistake moving out of Argentina because, at that point, I realized Americans are insane."

"Uh, yeah," I agreed. "About sports, we *definitely* are."

"Well, Sofia, my ex, pointed out to me on the ride home that football fans in South America—or, I guess you call it soccer—aren't exactly tame or sane."

"Also true."

She sighed happily and looked at her watch. "I better go check on Lucian. He slipped off after lunch without saying anything. Thanks for saving my ass. The Devil is stirring the shit today," she groaned with a shrug of her impeccably arched brows.

"No problem," I smiled. "See you at four, I guess."

"See you at four," she echoed, and tossed her apron on the island before leaving the kitchen with a short wave.

Her words replayed in my head as I pulled off my own apron and laid it carefully across the tile.

The Devil is stirring the shit today...

If everyday was as much of a roller coaster as this one had been so far, I was liable to go crazy—or, crazier than I already was coming in...and the day wasn't even done yet.

CHAPTER 9

THE GIVER

Between lunch cleanup and dinner prep, I went back to my

cabin in hopes of finding some different clothes to wear to dinner, but no

such luck. I took a nap, the day's onslaught of emotional ups and downs

having worn me out, and woke up just in time to head back to the kitchen

for round three of the day.

Thankfully, much to Catalina's elation, the refrigerator was stocked to the brim with fresh ingredients. She pulled them out by the greedy armful to examine them and decide what to use them in.

"Mangoes!" she squealed. "Cilantro! *Mmmm...*"

Shoving the bouquet of herbs under her own nose, she purred enthusiastically as she inhaled its aroma, then waved it under mine so I could do the same. Then, upon seeing further ingredients, she flung the bundle of cilantro on the island and turned back to the fridge.

"Fresh corn...grapefruit..." she listed off as she handed each item back to me. *"Aji amarillo!"* A pile of chile peppers rolled around the island —she was moving too fast for me to keep up.

She gasped, throwing her hands over her mouth and freezing like a statue.

"What? Don't tell me there's a dead body in there. I can't handle anymore gifts today," I joked.

"Well, it is a gift, and it's a dead body of some kind," she murmured, scooping the final ingredient out of the bottom of the fridge, and turning back to me with a wide smile and sparkling eyes. "Just not human."

A large, silver-scaled fish lay cradled in her arms, looking to be nearly three feet long. It glistened in the fluorescent lights as she gently laid it on the tiled kitchen island as if it were a small child or injured animal.

"Fish," I said. "Cool."

"*¡Carajo! Mina*...this is corvina," she corrected me, slipping into her native tongue in her excitement. "I can make ceviche!"

"That's great!" I replied with a smile. "You think everyone else will be cool with raw fish?"

"Fuck them," she stated affirmatively. "This afternoon was obviously a test, we passed, and this is our reward. I'm claiming it, and if any of those idiots has a problem, they can make themselves avocado toast. If I leave any avocados, that is..." she added with a mischievous smirk, looking up at me from under her thick, black lashes.

"Works for me," I laughed. "What do you want me to do?"

Catalina gave me instructions on what to chop and dice and peel and cook while she scaled and fileted the corvina with the care and precision of a surgeon. While she combined the ingredients like a mad scientist in a laboratory, I baked tortilla chips from the fresh tortillas that appeared with the rest of the ingredients and sliced a fresh baguette to make crostinis, as well. I watched her any time I could get a break from my tasks. She looked like a five-star chef, her eyes intensely surveying each leaf of cilantro and grain of coarse salt and splatter of lime juice as she put the finishing touches on the ceviche, which she plated beautifully in stemless martini glasses on little wooden boards, each garnished with an extra lime wedge and a sprig of cilantro.

"What time is it?" she asked when she finished.

Scanning the walls of the kitchen, I found the clock above the office door. "Five after five," I announced.

"*Bueno*," she murmured. "They should all be seated then. Grab a tray."

"A tray?" I echoed in question.

"You don't think I am putting my beautiful masterpiece on that stupid buffet table, do you?" she scoffed.

"Oh, of course not," I responded with a grin. "Table service it is then. Table service from St. Louis Slut Barbie and a five-star chef."

Catalina snorted her laughter through her nose and smirked as she loaded up a tray with the perfect dishes. "Did you come up with that, or was it our resident comedian?"

"The comedian, right after I pushed him out of the way of the beer tap."

A trill of laughter pealed from her lips as she hoisted her full tray carefully off of the island, and I did the same with mine, preparing to take them to the waiting diners.

"Well, here we go," she declared with a quick shrug of her eyebrows.

As we strode toward the table, where everyone was seated wearing looks of confusion, a few cat calls erupted and I tried my best to ignore them—a skill I was practiced in. Todd averted his eyes from me awkwardly, but the older men didn't take theirs away, and Didi's turned to daggers that narrowed in on my attire with pure loathing.

"Oh, that's a cute bra," Tracie cooed in a timid, but sweet, voice. Tracie seemed to be the type to always say something nice and make everyone feel comfortable. It was rather pleasant. I didn't understand it, and rarely, if ever, engaged in the behavior myself—but it was pleasant.

"Thank you, Tracie," I chuckled as I placed her dish in front of her.

"Yes, nice bra, Mickey," Bob chimed in.

"Bob!" Tracie gasped, using her elbow as an implement for reprimand against his side.

"What? You can say it but I can't?" he rebutted.

She shook her head at him and I suppressed a laugh, pursing my lips together as they curled up in an amused smirk. When all the plates were served, Catalina and I took the last two and sat in the remaining seats at the table, herself to the right of Lucian and myself to Todd's left.

"*Bon appetit!*" Catalina said with pride and exhilaration.

"Uh, what the fuck is it?" Herb uttered.

"It's ceviche," Todd answered, pouring me a glass of wine from one of the bottles on the table. Didi watched with a disapproving glare.

"Right, I know what ceviche is because I spent all my time before this dining at restaurants that serve things in martini glasses," Herb retorted sarcastically. "Fucking idiot."

"Is this raw fish?" Tracie asked, holding up a cube of the corvina between her fingers.

"Ceviche is a South American dish that usually features raw fish—yes, Tracie," Catalina explained.

"Well, it looks beautiful, ladies," Todd said with a smile at both of us before digging into his portion with a tortilla chip.

"It looks amateurish," Didi sighed as she eyed hers, appearing unenthused. "Ceviche in cocktail glasses is so 2013. I'd rather have a cock...tail," she added, her pause deliberate, a sultry gaze fixed on Todd.

"Well, then go make one, Didi," Todd snapped without looking at her, continuing to shovel in his food. "I'm eating."

"Catalina, it looks very pretty, so I'll give it a shot...but I don't usually eat raw fish," Trace said.

"I've taken her to a dozen sushi restaurants," Bob said with a laugh, "and she always gets California rolls and chicken teriyaki."

"This is fucking delicious!" Herb announced, lime and fish juices dribbling from his lips and streaking through his beard when he did.

Scooping some of my ceviche onto a chip, I took my first bite, closing my eyes to revel in the ecstasy of flavors—the tang of the lime, the punch of the cilantro, the nectar of the mango. The corvina practically melted in my mouth, and I couldn't stifle the moan that tumbled from my throat as it did. When I opened my eyes, almost everyone was staring at me, including Catalina, whose jaw gaped slightly while one eyebrow inched up her smooth forehead.

"It's really good," I squeaked in embarrassment, and her lips went from agape to pursed and curled in delight.

"*Gracias*," she said softly.

"So, Mickey," Herb barked, revealing a mouthful of dinner, "we missed you at breakfast and lunch, and in between. You figure it out yet?"

I nodded and took a drink of my wine, a crisp, effervescent white that paired almost perfectly with the taste profile of the ceviche. "I did. Porn and booze, huh?" I teased him.

The table erupted in raucous laughter.

"Oh, I see your buddy Todd has told you my secret," he chuckled.

"It's not a secret, Herb," Todd replied. "You tell everyone."

"You really sold your soul to the Devil for porn and booze?" I giggled. Catalina giggled next to me, holding her hands over Lucian's ears.

"I was homeless," Herb stated, as if it were a logical answer to my question.

"Why didn't you sell your soul for a home then?" I asked.

He stared at me as if II had asked the dumbest question he had ever heard.

"Well I got one, didn't I?" he rebutted, and the table broke out into laughter again. "And the booze, *and* the porn. The porn was pretty good, too."

"*¡Carajo!* My God! Enough about porn, Herb!" Catalina howled in mock protest. "There's a child present—I'm laughing too hard to hold his ears any longer!"

"That probably excludes a few of us from recounting our pasts then," Todd said.

"Definitely me," I agreed.

"Aren't you lucky, then?" Didi drawled sarcastically.

"Lucky that my past isn't suitable material to discuss in front of a child?" I snapped, quickly growing tired of her petty, jealous shit. "Hardly."

Tracie, in true peacekeeper fashion, awkwardly interjected: "We were the first ones, Bob and I."

"What did you sell your souls for?" I asked.

"A cruise."

An orchestra of hysterics sounded in the dining room.

Todd leaned toward me a bit, wheezing as he tried to wrangle the involuntarily guffaws that shook his entire body, tears of laughter in the corners of his eyes. "God, that one never gets old."

Catalina insisted we leave the dishes for the morning. I was surprised but didn't argue. She hung out in the lounge for drinks for a bit, laughing and happy, which seemed to catch everyone off guard at first, but by the time she left to put Lucian in bed at ten o'clock, everyone seemed more than used to it.

When Catalina left, I flopped onto a sofa by the stage, my feet finally alerting me that I had abused them with too much standing that day. Vivienne sat next to me and offered me a glass of wine, which I took.

"*Bonjour*," I tried my hand at the tiny bit of French I remembered from high school. "Or, no, hold on—*bonsoir*. Right? Is that right?"

She looked at me and silently shook her head, holding a finger to her full, flawless lips.

"Oh, okay," I muttered. "No talking. *Je suis ferme la bouche*. I'm sure that's wrong."

Vivienne rolled her eyes and let her head fall back for added drama.

"Sorry," I whispered with a shrug.

I sat with her for several minutes, not talking, just watching the interactions between the rest of them as if I were a people-watcher at an airport or a swimming pool—as if that were a hobby of mine, which it wasn't. But it was mildly fascinating. I had never really done it before.

Jeff and Jeric played darts with Didi. Their body language and facial expressions completely changed when they spoke to her as opposed to when they spoke to each other. To them, rough-cut and strong as oxen, she was a delicate flower. They were knights, and she was a damsel. Even though I personally didn't think she deserved it, they had taken it upon themselves to keep chivalry alive, despite the fact that we were all stuck on this stupid fucking cruise ship from hell. It was sort of admirable. Pointless, I thought, but admirable.

Herb and Tracie played backgammon, both with looks of intense focus on their faces that I never would have expected from my initial perceptions of them—Herb the whacky old man and Tracie the sweet empty-nester next door. Bob, usually demulcent and reserved in tone and mannerism, verbalized and gesticulated wildly at the bar for Todd, who nodded occasionally as he watched in profound amusement with his typical smirk and his arms crossed in front of his chest. He seemed to be reenacting an exciting football play, and when he finished, they both engaged in a mockery of a rowdy crowd, pumping their fists in the air and chanting a name I couldn't make out over the music.

Seeing everyone else so lively and engaged made me realize how exhausted I was. I didn't have to stretch my imagination to fathom why Catalina never hung out after dinner with everyone. We had been on our feet all day in that kitchen. I was used to it, as it was how a typical day at Mozzarella Mitch's went for me, and I generally came home and passed out after that and had nothing resembling a life outside work. Taking my last sip of wine and placing it on the table in front of the sofa, I turned to Vivienne. *"Merci beaucoup."*

"*Je vous en prie*," she replied with a polite nod. Her voice was nothing like I expected it to be, thinking it would be aged, or hoarse from lack of use. But it was sweet and rich, higher in pitch than mine, like the upper octaves of a perfectly-tuned grand piano, but not the highest ones that sounded tinny and reverberated in the ears.

She sounded like a fucking Disney princess.

I didn't want to attempt to say anything else and potentially annoy her as she had closed her eyes and let her head rest on the back of the sofa, enjoying the song that had just come on, which I recognized as a song from *Les Miserables*. With a final scan of the lounge to make sure I could slip out without having to engage in a round of good-nights, I left, headed for my room and bed.

Upon entry, I noticed the suitcase of skimpy clothes was gone and, thankfully, replaced with a plain white tank top and flannel pajama pants. I slipped into them, grateful for one split second as I slid into the sheets, but the thought of what might await me in the morning if Lucifer was in the gift-giving mood again kept me awake as I tried to fall asleep. After what felt like hours of restlessness, even though it had only been about forty minutes, a soft tapping sounded at my door at precisely midnight.

Hauling myself out of the comfort of the sheets, I trudged to the door and answered. Light poured in from the hallway, silhouetting the figure in front of me on a background of crisp, blue-toned incandescence, but I knew who it was by the outline. Short hair with slapdash spikes, shoulders and arms rippled with a hint of definition, standing about four lanky inches taller than myself.

"Todd," I whispered, my eyes squinting against the bright hallway. "What's up? Is everything okay?"

"Can I come in?" Todd asked, his voice tight and anxious.

"Sure." I stepped back and gestured for him to come through, then fumbled in the dark to flick on the desk lamp. He closed the door behind him and turned back around to face me just as I pivoted away from the desk.

My eyes flickered instantly to his hands, which nervously clutched and fiddled with something small, then back to his face which displayed a level of trouble and tension I didn't think possible from such a seemingly carefree guy.

"I just got back to my room, a minute ago," he muttered. "You're not the only one who got a gift today."

Turning up one hand and extending it toward me, he held the little package as if it were a venomous spider or a weapon.

Because, to him, it was. Shivers crawled across my skin as I took in the tiny bag, white dust settled at its bottom, a curled red ribbon securing the top as if it were a bag of bake sale cookies or Christmas candies.

"Todd..." I breathed.

"He's never given it to me before," he stated, staring at the baggie of cocaine in his hand with a mix of repulsion and need. "Always to someone else. Usually to Didi. Making me crawl to her, do whatever she said, whatever she wanted, because...because I can't—I can't—"

"I know," I murmured as comfortingly as I could manage given comforting others was not my forte, nor even a part-time hobby.

"Get it away from me, Mickey," he begged, his eyes shifting up to mine, imploring me for help. "Just take it—"

"Okay," I agreed, nodding as I closed the distance between us and grabbed the bag out of his hand. "Okay."

"Hide it, destroy it—I don't care," he continued, his voice breaking. "I don't want to see it, I don't want to think about it..."

"Okay," I repeated, stroking his shoulder gently to console him. "Todd, if I hide it, are you going to go look for it?" I asked in a sympathetic whisper.

He swallowed hard and his eyes burned into mine. "I don't want to," he replied. "I don't want to do it."

"I just wanted to know, so I can figure out how to help you."

"He's going to do it again," Todd rasped. "He'll just keep doing this to me until he fucking breaks me. It's been over six weeks since the last one."

"Why do you think he's doing it now?" I asked, tilting my head at him, slipping the cocaine in the pocket of my flannel pajamas.

He shrugged and scratched his head. "I have no fucking clue. Maybe because I just got to the point where I thought I had moved on," he said, ending his musing with an ironic laugh. He wandered to the bed and sat down slowly, then buried his head in his hands. "Fuck!"

"Todd, it's okay."

"I don't want to do it anymore! I don't want to do it!"

"I know you don't," I murmured. "That's why I'm gonna go get rid of it, okay? Give me five minutes."

I started to walk to the door, and he shot up off the bed and lightly grabbed my wrist.

"Don't go," he uttered softly, almost pleading.

I turned back to him. "You asked me to hide it, Todd."

"I know, but I know what he's doing. He's making me choose."

"Choose?" I echoed, my brows furrowing in confusion.

He nodded and took a step closer. "Between the old drug and the new." Taking the side of my face with his other hand, he stepped in another inch, and my breath caught in my chest.

"Did you just call me your new drug?" I scoffed in a breathless whisper.

His thumb stroked my cheekbone and the warmth of his exhale made my skin prickle.

"Maybe?" he shrugged playfully, running his other hand up my arm. I shuddered and my body took over for my mind, propelling my arms out to grab the waist of his jeans. His inhale shattered and hands trembled.

"Huey Lewis would be proud, I'm sure," I joked, and he choked on a laugh.

He slipped a hand in the pocket of my pajamas, clutched the bag of cocaine and drew it out without taking his eyes off mine. "I don't want to do this shit." He tossed it on the desk.

I nodded slowly and bit my lip.

"I want to do what we started earlier today," he murmured, grabbing my face in both hands and drawing me in until our lips met. As he took the kiss deeper, he enveloped me in his long arms, and I let my body melt into his as we pressed together.

He broke his lips from mine and pulled back just enough to give me a devilish, seductive smirk. "But if you want to keep me up all night like that would, I'm totally fine with that."

CHAPTER 10

PLEASE GET ME OUT OF HERE

He stayed that night. He stayed every night for the next week. I'd wake up with his arm wrapped over my side and the rustle of his breath against my shoulder. A few nights we didn't do anything but talk and joke and cuddle, but most nights....most nights we did things.

During the days, we tried our best not to let on to the others what went on in my cabin each night. Thankfully, I had one of the most demanding and time-consuming jobs on the ship, so I didn't even get the chance to interact with him much, or anyone for that matter, until after dinner clean-up. That was typically when his bartending duties kicked up a notch, so keeping things casual in front of everyone had been relatively easy, just by circumstance and without any special effort on our parts.

The pool shimmered in pleasant ripples in the sunlight on the main deck where I sprawled across a pastel-striped double lounger, covered partially by its tattered pink canopy. I tucked my white tank up into my bra to let the yellow warmth kiss my midsection, and had stripped down to my underwear, but covered that area with a towel, just in case someone happened along.

Lunch had gone smoothly that day. In fact, most meals had gone smoothly, though Catalina's jubilance and socializing had died down again after ceviche night. Cleanup had gone quickly since we had made BLTs and potato salad, which took fewer vessels and utensils to prepare than our usual kitchen endeavors, hence, less dish time. My first instinct when we finished up around twelve-thirty was to head to the lounge for a drink, but I refrained, fearing I might let it show that I wanted more than a beer from the bartender.

Somewhere in my wandering, looking for a spot to relax, I ran into

Herb who informed me the pool was "sparkling clean and pH-balanced".

Lucky for me, no one else was around when I showed up on the main deck, and I'd had the place to myself for a solid thirty minutes. My thighs glistened with the evidence of my quick dip into Herb's perfect pH water, but for the most part I had been enjoying the sunshine and solitude.

Lying on my side, propped up on one elbow, I succumbed to an old habit—one that felt simultaneously as routine as brushing my teeth and as foreign as a half-memory from a different life.

I checked my Facebook.

I didn't have many friends on it. Mostly some old college classmates I kept in touch with—watching in secret loathing and jealousy as they embarked on the journeys of their chosen careers or traveled around the world on their parent's dime—and a few of the girls from work that I could tolerate.

I smirked as I got an idea. Tapping away on the screen, I typed:

Please, someone get me out of here—I accidentally sold my soul to the Devil and now I'm on a crappy cruise ship where he plays with us like Barbies on a dream yacht! Help!

For extra entertainment, I added a picture of my feet, making sure to get as much of the worn down, derelict deck in the background as I could. I giggled in anticipation as I hit the 'post' button, eager to see what it would say—because it sure as shit wasn't going to say what I wrote.

The screen of my phone swirled and blurred, and when it came back into focus, I saw my post. Edited, of course, by Lucifer himself.

There was the picture of my feet, but the background had changed to a picturesque sunset over a grand deck full of beautiful people, a palmy, emerald island in the near distance. The picture had a simple caption, nowhere near the length of my original post.

Best decision I ever made.

I barked a singular, icy laugh and yelled "Fuck you!" before tossing the phone off the lounge and out of my sight.

"Everything okay?" came Todd's voice from behind me. I flopped on my back and arched my neck to look at him upside down.

"The Devil is a dickhead," I stated plainly.

Todd chuckled and I noticed one of his arms was tucked behind his back. "What happened?" he asked, shielding his eyes from the bright sun with his free hand and squinting at me.

"Nothing important," I answered. "He thinks he's being clever with his edits to my social media posts."

"You got on Facebook, hm?"

"Yes, and I thought he would change it to something funny."

"Something like 'I'm on a cruise, bitches!' and you wearing a grass skirt and drinking an impossibly giant margarita?"

"Yes! That's exactly what I was expecting! Instead he's just being a jerk," I pouted facetiously.

"Mickey, he *is* the Devil," Todd laughed. "I mean, I don't think he'd have the street cred he does if he wasn't a bit of a jerk every now and again."

"Anyway, enough about him," I sighed, bringing my neck back into normal alignment and wiggling in the lounger a bit to get comfortable again. "What's behind your back?"

Todd walked around to the front of the chair and sat down, brandishing a huge, tropical-looking cocktail, pink and orange and decorated with practically every garnish from the bar—a cherry, an orange twist, a pineapple chunk and, of course, a little paper umbrella. I shot up instantly.

"I thought you might like a nice cold beverage with your relaxing by the pool," he said as he handed it to me. I clasped the frosty glass in my hands.

"How did you know I was relaxing by the pool?" I asked, taking the straw in my lips.

"Don't laugh," he grinned and feigned embarrassment, "but I actually didn't. I just looked everywhere else for you first. I was kind of hoping you'd be in your room."

I cocked my head at him and adopted a demure grin. "Why's that?"

"Because everyone besides the two of us is at a planning meeting for my party..." he purred, running a hand over my thigh.

"I see," I murmured.

"So you probably don't need this anymore," he stated, flipping the towel off and tossing it to the back of the lounger. He surveyed the lower half of me with hungry eyes, his lip tucked into his teeth. "Okay, you don't need this either."

He took the drink away and set it on the ground behind him.

"Hey, you just gave me that!" I protested.

"You'll get it back in five minutes," he declared before plunging his lips against the crook of my neck.

"Five minutes?" I teased. "That's all?"

"Fine. Ten," he growled into my collarbone.

In an instant, I was lying on my back again, Todd hovering over me on all fours as his hands and lips explored my body. I closed my eyes, arched my spine, and let out a soft moan of satisfaction when his mouth found the thin skin covering my hip bone. His fingers slipped into the waist of my panties and I writhed in expectancy

"What the fuck is this?!" a shriek sounded behind us.

Todd scrambled backward and I shot up and whipped around. Didi stood a few feet away, hands on her hips and furious rage in her false-eyelash-framed eyes.

"Didi, what are you doing up here?" Todd spat.

"I was about to ask you the same thing," she snarled. "What exactly are you doing?"

"My life is none of your business," he snapped.

"Isn't it though?" she taunted, pulling something from the pocket of her tight red capri pants.

The red curled ribbon. My heart flipped.

"Get out of here," Todd growled his warning.

"I was going to tell you I had a present for you this morning, Toddy," she pouted facetiously, sauntering closer to us, her hot pink sarong shifting with her hips and her blonde topknot bun bouncing with each step. "Seems you found a new supplier."

"She's not a supplier, Didi," he rebutted. "I actually like her. And I don't want to do that shit anymore."

"*Like* her?" Didi scoffed, bending over under the ruse of scooping up the tropical drink Todd made me, but I suspected the maneuver was primarily intended to showcase her surgically perfected cleavage. "*Her*? This scrawny thing? Darling Toddy, just come back to mommy like a good boy and I won't punish you for whatever indiscretions you've partaken in with this...maroon-haired slut."

Heat—raging, coursing infuriated steam—built in my core and rushed through my skin. My jaw and fists clenched of their own volition.

"That's enough, Didi!" Todd barked. "I said get the fuck out of here."

"Alright, alright," she tittered playfully. "I *will* punish you...if you insist."

"Jesus fucking Christ," Todd groaned. "Aren't you supposed to be in the party planning meeting? You know, the thing you're in charge of?"

"We got to the menu and realized we were missing half of the kitchen," she answered. "The Argentine Terror refused to commit to my requests without clearance from her other half. So, I came looking for *her*. Want me to tell them you're...*busy*?"

"No," I snapped. "I'm coming."

"Not today, you're not," Didi laughed.

"God, Mickey, I am so sorry," Todd muttered in my ear. "I don't understand—"

"It's fine, it's not your fault," I mumbled as I stood from the lounger and searched for my pants.

"Looking for these?" Didi chirped with pride. She pointed at the ground and my eyes darted quickly down to see the wad of denim perched precariously at the edge of the pool, her toes nudging them closer and closer.

"Don't—" I started, but as soon as I moved to grab them, she flicked them into the water with her foot.

"Oops," she shrugged and took a sip of the tropical drink. "Aw, but don't you look just like something out of a Girls Gone Wild video? Satan's Spring Break! How's this tagline: Sad twenty somethings who wish they were still illegal."

"I'm about thirty seconds from slapping the fuck out of your plastic face," I declared, crossing my arms in front of my chest.

She gasped and dramatically clutched her chest, which was adorned with actual pearls. "Are you going to let her speak to me like this, Toddy Bear?"

"Absolutely," he said behind me.

She stared at me for a few moments in silence, her eyebrows and lips contorting as she seemed to be trying to manufacture an appropriately snarky reply. Apparently, she found one, because her face lit up.

"You know what this cruise ship needs?" she mused, cocking her head at me.

"A padded cell?" I offered.

"A wet t-shirt contest," she sneered, and before I had time to react, she poured the tropical drink over my head, her pomegranate lips peeled back into a vicious smile as the pink, sticky liquid gushed over my hair and face, and down my neck, settling on my chest.

"What the fuck, Didi!?" Todd yelled. Within a second, he was at my side, patting my neck and chest with the towel.

"Everyone is waiting on you, *sweetie*," she snarled at me before whipping around and heading back inside.

"Jesus—Todd!" I shouted, throwing my arms out to the side in bewilderment.

"I'm so sorry about this—God, Mickey, I'm—"

"You didn't tell me she was fucking insane and all...territorial for your dick!" I snapped at him.

"I didn't know she would be like *that*!" he argued, continuing his desperate attempts to towel dry me.

I snatched the towel away. "Would you stop that? Look at me! I'm not going to that meeting in my fucking underwear, Todd."

"I was just trying to help," he explained.

"You know what would really help?" I posited. "Not getting me involved in some bullshit romantic triangle with a rejected cast member of Real Housewives of Loonyville!"

"That was very poetic," Todd smirked and stifled a laugh in his throat.

"I'm fucking serious!"

"I know! I know—I'll talk to her, I—"

"Don't," I cut him off. "Don't go talk to her. She'll just wave cocaine in front of your face before sinking in her acrylics."

He crossed his arms and tilted his head. "You don't think I can resist the temptation?"

"I don't know if you can or not, Todd," I groaned, turning away and dropping to my knees to fish my pants out of the pool. "And I don't want to be the reason you put yourself in a position where it's there at all."

"How fucking thoughtful of you," he drawled sarcastically. "Is that to save yourself from guilt, or because you think since I asked you for help once that you're my goddamn sponsor? Either way, I don't think you actually give one shit about *me* in this instance."

I shot up from my kneeling position and rounded on him.

"You know what? Fuck off," I said.

"Fuck off? That's it?" he asked.

"Yeah, that's it. Fuck off. Go talk to Didi. Go do a line off her giant fake tits for all I care. I'm getting the fuck out of here."

I brushed past him and stormed toward the railing.

"What the hell are you doing?" he asked, following me.

I didn't respond or look back, just crawled up and over the railing.

"Mickey, stop—"

He rushed toward me, but not fast enough to stop me from jumping.

CHAPTER 11

A HUNDRED HOURS OF SOLITUDE

Cool water slapped my skin with a thousand salty hands, then commenced the slow and steady downward tug, enveloping me in its briny blanket. A powerful frog-like kick thrust me back above the surface and I could see the beach, a decent swim from my position, but nothing I couldn't handle. With perfect butterfly strokes and my eyes shut tight against the invasion of the salt water, I progressed to the sandy shelf until

I could stand.

Up on the beach, the shimmering golden granules clung to my wet feet and ankles. I whipped around and looked up at the deck—Todd was nowhere to be seen.

"He better not have jumped in after me," I muttered as I plopped down on the beach, then reclined back onto my elbows.

The lounger definitely had the comfort advantage, I thought, but the disadvantage of the other passengers, which today was a major one. I sighed and shook my head, though I didn't know why. No one was around to see me. Unless...

"Is this what you wanted?" I asked out loud. "You wanted me to get mixed up with...with the cute comedian with a secret soft side and a dark past, and his psycho, Stepford wife sugar mama? Well, you win. I hope you're entertained! Wanna see my tits, too?!" I added in a shout, cupping my mouth to aid the volume.

The only sound was the constant shush and swish of the waves.

"Oh, who the fuck am I kidding, you've already seen my tits. So, what's next?"

I had to go back at some point. I would starve if I didn't. But, when I went back, I'd have Didi hellbent on tormenting and punishing me for taking her plaything, I'd have Todd wanting to *talk*, and I'd have the whole group ticked off that I held up their meeting.

And I'd have no pants.

Groaning, I let every muscle in my body release, flopping completely on my back in the warm sand. Catalina would be angry. Hopefully not after I explained to her what Didi did to me on the deck, and how I couldn't stand to show my face—or more like my half-naked, sugar-coated body—in front of everyone.

A pang of guilt settled deep in my stomach. She had valued my feelings and input enough to make everyone wait for me, and then I tossed myself overboard and left her to deal with the aftermath. Hopefully, she didn't take it personally. Hopefully, she told Didi to fuck off and cook her own goddamn party menu. Suddenly, I wanted back on the cruise ship as soon as possible so I could go do it myself.

"Didi," I said, as if she were right in front of me, "make your own food, you stuck up bitch."

A seagull squawked loudly in the air above me.

"That's right, Didi, you heard me," I shouted at the seagull, pretending it was Didi, squawking in speechless protest. "Your parties are stupid—well, they're probably stupid, I haven't been to one yet—no, don't say that. Your parties are lame and I'm not cooking for your lame party, and neither is Catalina! And ceviche is *awesome*, you spoiled twat!"

The seagull swooped low briefly and let out a series of screaks and caws that sounded like laughter before rising high into the sky and disappearing.

"Fuck you, too," I muttered, shielding my eyes against the sun as I watched the white wings fade into the wispy cotton clouds. "Jesus, I came here to get away from everyone and ten minutes in I'm talking to a fucking seagull."

I didn't want Todd to do that cocaine.

I didn't want Catalina to feel like I abandoned her.

I didn't want to care about these people like I already did, after a mere week and half. It felt like defeat. It felt like resignation to the idea that I'd be stuck on that ship for months, or years.

"Maybe...maybe I'll just stay out here," I said aloud.

Closing my eyes against the sun, noticing the warm ache of exertion in my muscles and the tingle of salt in my skin, I drifted off to sleep on the beach.

A squawk sounded behind me, my alarm to wake from my nap. My eyes shot open and I didn't have to squint against the sun as it was no longer directly above me. Judging by its movement in the crystal blue sky, I had napped almost three hours.

"Shit," I groaned. "Dinner prep."

The bird call rang out across the beach again, and I realized it was a bit higher pitched and clearer than the gull's squawks. And it sounded like it came from the ground and not the clouds...

I rolled over to my stomach and looked at the small patch of palm trees at the center of the island.

"Caw-maw!" The sound came again, and I finally saw its source—a scarlet macaw perched in an umbrella tree. "Cawm awn!"

I scrunched my face and cocked my head. "Come on?"

"Yeeaaahhh! Come on!"

"What the actual fuck..." I rasped as I crawled my feet up under my body then stood.

Plodding through the sand, enjoying the slight tickle as it shifted around each foot with each step, I kept my eye on the macaw as I neared the forested area. But, as soon as I was under his tree, he flew deeper into the ring of palms. I took a few steps further in and did a double take. The jungle I stood in was suddenly massive, an emerald-tinted city of foliage, teeming and buzzing with life and vibrance. Taking several steps backward, I found myself looking at ten sparse palm and umbrella trees, which hardly provided decent shade, let alone the thick, lush canopy I had just seen.

I stepped back under the umbrella tree and was immediately transported to the oasis, beautiful yet slightly eery with its green tint. The pool at its center sparkled as if by magic, and a leopard stooped low at its mossy bank with pink tongue extended, ready to lap it up. Upon hearing my approach, signaled by the crunch of moss under my weight, the leopard stopped drinking and looked in my direction.

"What up, bitch?" he asked in a low voice with a casual jerk of his head.

"I—excuse me?" I coughed.

"Oh, excuse *me*," he drawled sardonically with a roll of his feline eyes. "Good afternoon, madame."

"Well, aren't you cheeky?" I remarked, fairly certain at this point that I had drowned and this was all my brain's final dream dump. "Also, I'm not a madame."

"Whatever," he growled, and turned to saunter away.

I clicked my tongue and crossed my arms in front of my chest when he finally disappeared into the jade shadows, his jutting feline hips shifting with each languid, prowling step. "What a dick."

Spinning in a circle, I took in my surroundings with tighter surveillance. Butterflies of all shapes, sizes, and colors daintily visited the bromeliads and orchids. Birds fluttered noisily amongst the array of green foliage. Mangoes, papayas, bananas and coconuts clung to their respective trees, eliciting an echoing digestive rumble and a surge of saliva from me. Apparently I didn't eat enough lunch.

But could I trust this fruit? This was obviously an elaborate mirage, another of the Devil's pranks or ploys.

"Or maybe I'm dead," I muttered again. "But if I'm dead, why am I hungry? Maybe I only think I'm hungry, like when you're peeing in a dream but you're not actually peeing in real life."

"Oh for fuck'ssssake, shut up and eat the fruit," came a voice behind me. I whipped around to find its source and noticed a little green snake wrapped around a coconut whose narrow mouth moved under my careful watch. "You're actually hungry. You're not dead, or dreaming."

"Great," I sighed. "I'm Doctor fucking Doolittle."

"Coconuts are really dense in nutrients," the chartreuse serpent continued his persuasion.

"Wait....wait!" I exclaimed in triumph. "Wait a fucking minute! A snake. Trying to get me to eat some fruit. Holy shit!"

"Holy sssssshit, indeed," he hissed slyly, adding a little wink at the end.

"Okay, I thought it was an apple in the Garden of Eden?" I said, cocking my head and taking a step through a sprawling jungle fern to get closer to the diminutive, reptilian Devil.

"Ssssunday Sssschool bullshit. It doesn't actually sssay anything in that book at all. Just that it was *forbidden* by the killjoy upstairssss." He jerked his slender head toward the canopy, but I knew he meant beyond that—quite a bit beyond that. "I guessss nobody felt like writing about how Eve broke sssome giant hairy ballsss and drank their glissstening milk. But I'm tellin' you, from what I sssaw, she did love the hairy ballsss and glistening—"

"Stop!" I interjected, and his lipless mouth spread into a wicked grin, his forked tongue darting around in satisfaction. "Stop, seriously. I get it."

"If coconutsss aren't your thing, have a mango. Or banana. Whatever. They're all mine. They'll all do the ssssame thing."

"And what's that?"

"Take you back," he answered.

"Back..." I breathed. "Back *where*?"

"Wouldn't be much fun if I told you that, would it?" he taunted, dropping down to the jungle floor and slithering toward me. Instinctively, I backed up a step and he laughed. "I'm not venomous."

"No, you're just Satan..." I grumbled, but I stopped my retreat and knelt down, holding out my hand for him, and soon he was wrapped around my wrist, staring at my face. "So, the stupid cruise ship, then, huh?"

"You're not done yet," he hissed with a serpentine grin. "None of you are."

"Done with what?" I asked, tilting my head in confusion.

"The puzzle," was his answer.

"Is this some stupid horror movie bullshit?" I spat. "Is this an escape room?"

"Sssssomething like that." He nodded his little snake head.

I sighed and dropped to my butt on the damp ground, rainforest moisture seeping into the thin cotton of my underwear. "You suck."

"Correction, I *bite*," he joked, bearing his fangs and winking. "Alssso, you literally would not have booze, comedy, basssic ssscientific knowledge, orgasmsss, Halloween, booksss about magic, rock 'n' roll, or the motherfucking internet without me, so how much do I suck now?"

"Until you let me off that cruise ship, still a lot," I answered. "I mean, thanks for all the cool shit. But you and I are not friends right now." I flicked my pointer finger back and forth between our faces.

"You have the power to get home," he teased.

"I swear to the 'killjoy upstairs', if this is some Wizard of Oz fuckery —"

"Give me a little credit, Missss Martin," he laughed, each raspy, reptilian chortle punctuated by a flick of his thin, flame red tongue. "It'sss a bit more complicated than that."

I growled in frustration and rubbed my forehead with my unoccupied hand. "Side note, you aren't slimy."

"Common misssconception."

"I like this smooth yet scaly thing. It's kind of nice. All snakes are like this?"

"Yep," he nodded.

"Cool," I nodded back.

"Are you trying to be friendly ssso I'll let you go home?" he asked.

I shrugged and exhaled a raspy sigh. "Maybe," I admitted.

"And you would jussst leave them?"

That familiar pang of guilt stabbed between my ribs, and despite my best efforts at hiding it, my face pulled with concern.

"Go help them. Take a bite...a juicy bite..."

"Alright! Stop with the Snow White routine. Jesus—"

"For the record, I had nothing to do with Jesusss. That was all your kind."

I rolled my eyes and traversed the oasis, the Devil still coiled around my wrist, until I found a bunch of mangoes nestled against a tree. When I plucked one from the group, my little green companion coughed loudly.

"I would wash that," he said. "Just sssaying."

No response or retort found me. All I could muster was a furrow of my brow and a disgusted curl of my lip as I plodded to the sparkling magic pool and knelt down, dipping the mango, a half-ripened swirl of shades of lime and orange, under its surface. I pulled it out, shook it off, then let out a long, loud exhale.

"Here goes nothing," I sighed.

My teeth met the skin, sinking into the tough flesh, drawing forth the nectar, and more and more nectar until it became too much for my mouth and it trickled from lips and down my chin.

The snake smiled, and his voice filled my ears as I went woozy and my knees buckled, sending me plummeting toward the pond in front of me.

"Sssssee you on the other ssssside..."

I awoke in my bed, lying on top of the covers, fully clothed in slim-fit dark denim jeans and a scarlet sleeveless blouse, ruffled along the neck line. Flame red snakeskin stilettos adorned my feet, and when I pulled my hand in front of my face to rub my forehead, I saw a thick silver bracelet on my wrist...

A coiled snake.

"Cute," I muttered.

Rolling off the bed, I sighed heavily. The clock on the wall read 5:00 on the dot. Catalina was surely finished with the majority of the dinner prep, but I felt obligated to at least go help in whatever way I could, and explain why I had jumped overboard during the meeting.

Maybe if I offered to do cleanup for the next few days, she'd get over me ditching the party planning business and dinner duty, I thought. Striding through the halls and ascending up to the main floor with jaunty steps, I prepared my statement to Catalina in my head.

When I entered the kitchen, her head snapped up from her task of garnishing enchilada pies with drizzles of sour cream sauce and chopped ribbon chives.

"That looks beautiful," I said.

She didn't move. Her eyes went wide. Then her jaw gaped.

"Is—fuck, did my tit fall out or something?" I asked, shifting my eyes down to check my appearance, as something about it was obviously catching her off guard. "Nope, okay. All good in that department. Look, Catalina, I'm really sorry about today, and I'm gonna do dishes for you—no, all the cleanup, and all the onion work, too—for the rest of the week."

Nothing. She remained a stone statue of a woman in shock.

"Um, do you want me to take those out to the buffet for you?" I offered awkwardly, walking around the island until I was standing next to her.

I reached across her for the first enchilada pie, her eyes fixated on me like I were Satan himself, or a giant talking serpent. My arm brushed against hers when I pulled the enchilada pie back toward me, preparing to take it out to the dining hall. She gasped.

"¡*Carajo!*" she uttered breathlessly, her hands framing her mouth in disbelief. "You are alive!"

I had just enough time to set the pie back down on the island before her arms wrapped around my neck and she squeezed me into a desperate embrace.

"Yes," I grunted against the constriction of her display of affection. "I am...very alive. Hence in need of oxygen. To breathe."

She pulled away and looked me in the eyes. "I was so worried about you," she whispered, squeezing my shoulders. "Everyone thought—I thought..."

"Catalina," I said, tilting my head slowly in confusion, "I don't know what the big deal is. Why would everyone think I was dead? Todd probably watched me swim to the shore—I was only gone for, like, four hours?"

Catalina shook her head. "No, Michaela," she murmured, brushing a tendril of hair from my face. My stomach flipped nervously. "You have been gone for four *days*."

CHAPTER 12

SNAKES ON A CRUISE

"First of all, *Michaela*?" I asked, crossing my arms.

Catalina pulled her hand away and dropped her eyes in embarrassment.

"I looked through your phone," she admitted.

"What? Why?"

"I don't know!" She threw her hands in the air, flustered. "We were trying to figure out if we could tell anyone and—and then I was just looking through some pictures because I missed you."

"You *missed* me?" I narrowed my eyes playfully. A smirk pulled at the corner of my lips.

"Yes," she replied, almost reluctantly. "Anyway, you got an email from your student loan company while I was looking at pictures of your senior trip to Manhattan. Miss Michaela Martin is officially done with her payments. And I'm glad I saw it, too, because I was growing quite annoyed with having to call you by that silly nickname. Your full name is beautiful."

"Well, when you say it, it is," I remarked. "But listen, Catalina, I swear —I went down there, I took a three hour nap, I talked to a snake, ate some fruit and I was back."

"Oh, he thinks he's cute, doesn't he?" she chuckled coolly and rolled her eyes.

I held my arm up between us so the silver serpent on my wrist was in front of her face.

"Clearly," I drawled. "*Precious.*"

"Well, I don't know what to tell you, Michaela," she murmured. "It has been four days and four hours since you jumped overboard."

"That's so fucking weird," I muttered, shifting and resting my rear against the island. "So, I'm guessing you know why I flipped out then?" I added, my face twisted in shame, my eyes imploring her for forgiveness.

"Todd did tell me about what happened right beforehand, yes" she responded. "I really don't blame you for wanting to get the hell out of here. Didi is...a piece of work. Though, I will admit, I was mad at you for leaving, and possibly dying, for selfish reasons."

"I know, I'm sorry," I whimpered. "I felt like shit that you had to do one meal on your own. Now I find out you've done a dozen! God, I promise, dish duty for a month—"

"That's not what I meant," she laughed. "I was lonely. I mean—I've gotten used to you in the kitchen, not just as a helping hand. As a friend. I don't really feel like I've connected with anyone on this stupid ship. And you were here a few days and I felt...I don't know. Comfortable. Excited to come to the kitchen, instead of dreading every single day that I woke up here."

A little spark, like from the click of the flint on a lighter, fizzled under my sternum.

"Anyway, let's get these out before they get cold, and we can come back in here and discuss the snake on this cruise over some Spanish Tempranillo Vivienne found in the wine cellar," Catalina instructed as she scooped up one of the dishes and headed for the dining area.

I started to follow her with the other enchilada pie, but stopped dead in my tracks as her words hit me.

"The snake on the cruise," I muttered.

She turned back and looked at me with a mix of concern and bewilderment.

"Michaela?"

"He said he'd see me on the other side, right before he sent me back here," I mumbled to myself.

She cocked her head. "You think he was saying...?"

"That he's actually *on* the ship?" I finished her thought with wide eyes. "Yes, I do."

"Holy shit!" she uttered, her eyes going wider than mine.

"Holy shit, indeed..." I echoed the snake's hissed words from the jungle oasis.

"As an actual snake? We'd never find him."

I bit my lip and shook my head, walking to the buffet table slowly, lost in thought. "I don't know. I don't think so. I think the snake routine on the island was all symbolic."

My head spun and I squinted and chewed my lip, trying to focus, trying to remember. I didn't even realize that eight people were closing in on me until it was too late.

"Jesus Christ!" Todd ejected, throwing his arms around me in a similar manner to Catalina in the kitchen. "Holy shit...holy—my God, you're alright," he murmured in my ear.

Over his shoulder, I caught a glimpse of Didi, giving me a death glare with her smoky, kohl-smudged eyes. I wondered briefly what happened between them in my hundred-hour absence, but shoved it out of my head, not wanting to get caught between them again.

"I'm fine," I assured him, pulling out of his hold slowly and patting him on the shoulder. "A pleasant relaxing day at the beach. A psychedelic jungle excursion. Just what I needed," I joked. "Really, you should all try it."

"How on earth did you survive without food or fresh water for *four days*?" Tracie uttered in breathless shock.

"Well, it helped that it was only four hours on my end," I chuckled. "And there was some food and water, courtesy of our benefactor himself."

"And you...you ate it?" Bob asked nervously.

I nodded.

"You eat food from him every day, Bob," Catalina laughed next to me.

Bob shrugged and his lips pulled down while his bushy brown brows crawled up his forehead. "When you put it that way..."

Jeric, usually a man of few words and outward expressions, slapped his hands on either side of his scruffy chin and barked: "Wait!"

All heads snapped to him.

"What?" Jeff asked his brother.

"If it was only four hours for you out there..."

He trailed off and stroked his beard, but Jeff's face lit up as he apparently followed his twin's unspoken thought. "Is it like that everywhere?"

"You mean, like...*home*?" Tracie asked.

"Yes," Jeff and Jeric said in unison.

We all exchanged looks of silent hope and wonder.

"That would explain why nobody is looking for us," Todd mused aloud with upturned hands. "Maybe we haven't actually been gone very long."

"If I was gone for four hours out there, but a hundred hours to you guys on the ship—"

"One hour in the real world is twenty five here," Catalina finished my sentence, her face flooded with relief and bright with a smile.

"Oh my god, that would mean I've only missed three shows of my tour," Todd muttered, looking deep in thought. "I could still salvage that, I'm sure..."

Everyone started buzzing amongst themselves, excited at the prospect that they hadn't missed as much of their lives outside the Devil's cruise ship as they originally thought. They kept up the hubbub as they fixed their plates and made their way to their seats. I watched it all in silence and waited until they had dispersed and started lively discourse at the table before I took a slice of the enchilada pie, put it on a plate, and handed it to Catalina.

"So, Tempranillo, hm?" I asked, pursing my lips playfully and raising my brows.

"A connoisseur?" she asked, cocking her head. "I thought it was only Vivienne and myself."

"It is," I laughed as I took a sliver of the pie for myself. "I am merely a lush."

She laughed lightly through her nose as she turned and headed back into the kitchen. I followed, watching her dark hair, which she kept up while cooking but left down most other times, swish back and forth across her shoulders, different shades of coffee and chocolate and black walnut shining in her locks depending on the angle of the light on them.

She was the first person I met on this ship—I never forgot that. She was also the first person I saw when I got back after the island...

See you on the other side...

I had chosen to go see Catalina, though, hadn't I? But, perhaps he would know that, I thought. Surely he just meant he was on the ship in general, not necessarily the *first* person I was going to see?

I couldn't convince myself Catalina was the Devil...but I knew I shouldn't rule it out. I shouldn't rule it out for any of them, no matter my personal feelings toward each individual. It was time to put up my guard and put it up hard.

"You made them really happy tonight, Michaela," Catalina murmured when we reached the kitchen, setting our plates down on the island.

The island, I thought with a shudder. I spent a huge amount of my time with her at this kitchen island, and my encounter with Satan as a serpent had happened on an island.

Okay, now you're stretching, Mickey, I admonished myself silently.

"Yeah, wait until they figure out that it means it's going to be a hell of a lot longer before anyone actually does come looking for us," I drawled sarcastically.

Catalina's face dropped and she swallowed her bite of food. "Oh, you're right."

It couldn't be her, I told myself. Her face was so open, so honest and innocent. Not in the naive way—almost imperceptible worry lines and shockingly sharp eyes proved she was both experienced and wisened—but in the way that makes a person a terrible liar. She was too genuine, or else I was too trusting, and possibly naive myself.

"Don't worry," I sighed. "That's not how we're getting out of here."

"What do you mean?" she asked, cocking her head at me again, her hair slipping all to one shoulder in a shimmering cascade of espresso. "What did he say?"

I cleared my throat, trying to remember the words from that scaly, spring green mouth, a clear visual of the flickering red tongue popping up with the memory when I did. "That's it's a puzzle, or...like an escape room. And we aren't done yet."

"What's an escape room?" Catalina questioned, her lips smooshed into a pucker and her brows furrowed.

I laughed, coughing on a bite of enchilada, knowing she would find the concept ridiculous. "Okay, so you go to this building with your friends and they lock you all in a room together, and you have to solve all these little puzzles to get out within the time limit," I explained with partially suppressed, screwy grin.

Her eyes went wide and incredulous, then she shook her head and clicked her tongue. "Americans," she sighed. "And you pay for this?"

"Yeah, it's like going to the arcade, or bowling," I chuckled. "It's supposed to be fun."

"Have you done this-this escape room business?"

"Me? No. I'm sort of wishing I had, though, now that we're kind of in one."

"This is popular amongst people your age?"

I shrugged and tilted my head back and forth as I considered the question. "Yeah, mostly my age group, probably."

"Well, we should find out if the other person in your age group has partaken in this activity, then," Catalina declared, matter-of-factly.

"Todd?"

She nodded at me, raising her eyebrows and shifting her puckered lips to one side.

"You can talk to him then. I'd rather keep my distance, lest I incur the wrath of Didi," I groaned, dropping my eyes in embarrassment and pretending to examine my food with my fork.

"Fine, I will talk to him," she agreed, her smooth voice a soft murmur. "For you."

When I looked up, she captured me in her intent gaze. My heart did a full 360 degree jump and my cheeks had to be the color of summer tomatoes.

"I'm going to go make sure Lucian ate enough dinner," she stated before swooping out of the kitchen, the swish of her hair resuming, to my delighted confusion.

"What the hell is going on?" I whispered to myself. At that moment, I really needed that wine she had mentioned.

Absentmindedly, I started the cleanup process in the kitchen, stacking dishes and carting them to the sanitizer with plodding, languorous steps that filled the kitchen with the echoing clicks and clacks of the snakeskin heels. It wasn't until I finished cleaning the whole kitchen by myself that I realized how long Catalina had been gone.

I had told her I would do dishes on my own for a month, so I wouldn't blame her for not coming back, but...I had gotten a vibe. I thought she was flirting with me. And the more I thought about it, as I wiped down the pink-tiled island with her vinegar and lemon juice mix, tonight wasn't the first time she'd flirted, or hinted.

And I wanted her to come back. Right in that moment, I wanted her back in my sight, back in the same room as me.

Why? I asked myself, my head buzzing and pulse racing, a sheen of sweat forming on the back of my neck, the palms of my hands, and between my breasts. I wasn't that hard up for attention. I'd had plenty from Todd, and in my 'real life', I had usually shied away from it. Given my previous longstanding profession, people being physically attracted to me wasn't generally noteworthy to me, unless...

My shoulders prickled and my breath caught. A familiar warmth sat atop my stomach, like a steaming mug full of nerves and want sitting on a shelf.

Unless I was attracted to them, as well.

The mug on the shelf began to boil, bubbling over, the nerves splashing over the rim and trickling down the sides. I tossed the cleaning rag onto the gleaming tiles and ran out of the kitchen, lumps of nerves forming in each and every place they saw fit—the rear of my throat, the bottom of my stomach, the nape of my neck, the bones of my hips.

En route to my room, and hoping not to encounter anyone on my way, I carefully sneaked into the lounge, stalking like some small predatory animal behind the bar to the mini-fridge that held bottled beers. Just as my fingers slipped around the handle to its door, I heard footsteps and voices coming toward me. Shifting from my crouch to a kneel, I quieted my breathing and froze as best as I could.

The jumbled, muffled words grew clearer as their speakers approached, and with the added clarity, I recognized the voices easily. They were both quite familiar to me by this point.

"Yes, I see what you're saying," Catalina's voice drifted from the hallway outside the lounge, just around the corner from the bar where I hid. "But I'm reserving judgment, and I think you should, as well."

"You're really saying you don't think it's odd that *she's* the one all of the sudden telling us it's a puzzle, like two weeks after showing up?" Todd rasped. "I mean, fuck, Cat. It's one thing to reserve judgment, but a completely different thing to withhold caution and question."

"It is questionable, alright?" Catalina retorted, keeping her voice low. My stomach churned. "This little Genesis Bermuda Triangle story is hard to grasp, I will admit—"

"Did you *see* her tonight?!" Todd interrupted.

"But, if we examine everyone, I'm sure we could come up with a compelling case," Catalina argued, ignoring his interruption. "And that's *exactly* what he wants! Todd, he wants to turn us against each other—to play on this paranoia and suspicion, so we never solve the puzzle and we never get out of here."

Todd sighed heavily. "I get it. I've seen you around her. You wanna ignore this because you want a girlfriend—"

"That's not what this is about."

"Whatever. You want to jump in bed with Devil, you do it."

My body trembled, my veins fizzling with bubbles and sparks of anxiety.

"I'm trying to remain logical here, Todd. And we have absolutely no evidence that points concretely at any individual on this ship. And, while you're accusing me of who I may or may not want to jump in bed with, one of your known partners may not be the actual Devil, but she's your own personal Devil. I'd mind your own affairs."

Todd sighed, then growled in agitation. "Whatever."

"If I were you, I would focus on not letting Didi sink her *pitchfork* in any farther," Catalina taunted in a low drawl.

"You let me handle Didi," Todd snapped.

"Then handle her," Catalina rebutted. "Because you haven't been before this. She has been handling you, quite easily."

"Anything else, Argentina?" Todd spat, his voice rippled with agitation.

"No, *no mas.*"

"Good. I have to get the bar ready."

My heart leaped and started pumping blazing hot adrenaline through every inch of my body. His footsteps made their way across the opposite side of the bar—in a matter of seconds he'd come around and find me—and the what would I do? What would I say? I panicked in frozen silence.

"I don't believe I saw you clean up your tray from dinner," Catalina said plainly.

Todd's footsteps stopped, he sighed, then the footsteps retreated back along their initial path.

Ice cold relief washed away the fiery dread as both of them left the lounge. I waited with bated breath until I was sure they were out of earshot before popping the bar fridge open, heart still pounding, and slipped my shaking fingers around the long necks of two amber ales. With my liquid prey finally in my grasp, I scurried back to my room like the spooked little animal I was.

Plopping my ass on my bed, emotionally drained from the roller coaster I had just ridden, I reveled in the hiss and crack from the beer as I twisted the cap from its station.

"God, what a fucking day," I groaned before partaking of the contents.

I swallowed. "Or four," I said in my beer voice.

"Long time, no talk," I replied.

"Well, you've had your shit together, for the most part," beer voice said. "Now you're a mess again. Lucky me."

"Yeah," I sighed. Another swig. "Lucky me..."

CHAPTER 13

THE DEVIL DUDE

Sleep in any form that could be considered beneficial eluded me

that night, and I woke to a hazy yellow light and crawling skin.

I didn't want to face Catalina, afraid my nerves would get the better

of me and render me useless. I didn't want to think about whatever these

feelings were that happened in her presence, and her absence.

I didn't want to be anywhere near Todd after the confrontation with

Didi, and after what I had heard the night before—his suspicions about me being the Devil in disguise.

Rolling over in the bed, prepared to pull the sheets over my head and not leave my room all day, an uncomfortable rigidity across my abdomen restricted my movement and a scratchy sensation covered my legs. I whipped the sheet off my body and looked down.

Red corset leotard. Red fishnet stockings attached with garters. Red kitten heels. Red elbow length gloves.

"You've got to be fucking kidding me," I groaned, hauling myself up to sit. "Not *again*."

The corset was sleeveless, trimmed with red feathers that brought the eye down to the cleavage it forcefully created. I stood and walked to the mirror on the back of my door. A giant red feather and two sparkly devil-horns poked out of an intricate updo atop my head. My face was overly made up in varying shades of scarlet and ruby, and cat eyes drawn in black liner damn near to my temples.

"Oh my god," I muttered, scanning my reflection in horror. "I look like a rejected version of Lola that haunts Barry Manilow's nightmares."

Now aware of my appearance, I *really* didn't want to see anyone today. Dejected and defeated, I spun away from the mirror to check the time, and a little red rectangle on the desk caught my eye. It was an

envelope and I snatched it up, ripping it open, hoping its sender had some

explanation for my ridiculous attire.

YOU'RE INVITED TO A BURLESQUE NIGHT TO CELEBRATE TODD'S

200TH DAY ABOARD THE CRUISE.

AND, IT'S EITHER THIS GET UP OR <u>NAKED</u>. DEAL WITH IT, SUGAR.

XOXO

YOURS TRULY,

SATAN, LUCIFER, THE ANGEL OF LIGHT, THE MORNING STAR, THE

BEAST, BEELZEBUB (THAT'S MY FAVORITE), LITTLE HORN (NOT

REALLY A FAN OF THAT ONE), RULER OF DEMONS, SERPENT OF OLD,

THE DEVIL DUDE

Burlesque. Of course, I thought. That had been Didi's idea on my first

day here.

"Fucking Didi," I muttered angrily through my teeth.

Fucking Didi, I thought, a light bulb clicking on in my head. My eyes shot up to the list of names he'd signed.

"The Devil Dude," I read aloud. "D. D."

Everything seemed to fall into place so easily...Didi had acted like she knew I was a stripper, before anyone else did, and certainly before I told anyone. And her taunting and controlling Todd with the cocaine seemed like such a Devil thing to do.

Plus, she was a total bitch.

My thoughts about Didi were interrupted by a blood-curdling shriek from somewhere on the ship. I wrenched my door open and ran, as best I could in the stupid kitten heels, toward the sound. One floor up, Tracie, Bob, and Todd gathered in the hall around Didi.

Fucking Didi.

She sobbed hysterically, wailing unintelligible words while Tracie tried to comfort her with shoulders rubs. As I approached, no longer concerned since I cared little for Didi's feelings, I noticed that everyone was dressed in similarly ridiculous red ensembles, though certainly none as risque as mine.

"This isn't what I wanted!" Didi bawled.

"This is exactly what you wanted," Todd retorted.

"But I changed my mind," she argued. "We decide to do a luau instead, didn't we?"

Tracie and Bob nodded.

"I never wanted Burlesque—it was a joke!" she cried. "Why is he doing this to my party?"

I couldn't stop the ironic snort that sounded from my nose and alerted the rest of them to my presence. They all turned and their eyes went wide in unison.

"Oh god, of course!" Didi shouted, throwing her hands in the air. "Of course, just another excuse for you to be the sexy one, and dress like a tramp, so that no one's paying attention to Didi!" She whipped a red handkerchief out of Bob's blazer pocket and loudly blew her nose.

"Well, you didn't have to dress me like this if you didn't want to," I sneered.

"*What*!?" she barked.

"Mickey, now is not the time—" Todd tried to intervene, but I held up my hand.

"Save it," I snapped. "I know you think it's me."

"We all think it's you!" Didi yelled, her ruby lips curling back to bear her perfect teeth like an aging showgirl lioness. "I mean *look*—you actually have devil horns on your head!"

"I didn't dress myself like this!" I matched her volume. "It's a fucking head band! Your name is Didi. Like two letter Ds. Like short for Devil Dude!"

"Devil Dude?" Todd tittered.

"On the note—the invitation," I replied. "The list of his names."

"Mine just said 'The Devil'," Tracie mumbled while her eyes darted between them all nervously.

"Mine, too," Todd said. He sauntered toward me slowly, adorned in a bright red three-piece suit, a white lily tucked in his breast pocket, his hair greased and combed neatly to one side, making him look like a big-shot mobster from the twenties. "So, you had some extra salutations on yours? What, 'cause you and the *Devil Dude* are such good buds since your little vacay in the Garden of Eden?"

I surveyed them all, their wary eyes boring into every inch of me like I were a wax figure in a haunted house—like I might suddenly pop out at them and do something terrifying.

"You know what, Todd. Fuck you. I have to go make your breakfast now. All of your breakfasts, you ungrateful jerks!" I shouted, then spun on my heels and stomped down the hallway and up the stairs to the main

deck.

Finding the kitchen empty upon my arrival, I grabbed a metal

mixing bowl and threw it frisbee style at the wall while roaring my ire

through my lips.

Turned out I wasn't alone. I heard a shuffle of papers and the rolling

wheels of a desk chair.

"Hey," Catalina poked her head out of the office. "Oh."

Her eyes flickered briefly as they engaged in a subtle but certainly

noticeable up and down of my appearance, then went back to normal, but

a slight curl of a smirk revealed her satisfaction...or possibly her

amusement.

"Rough morning?" she teased, standing from the chair and bringing

a handful of papers to the island. "It's only seven a.m."

I tried not to let my inspection of her Burlesque Night apparel show

in my eyes as they took in as much surface area of her as they could

before she looked up from her recipes and caught me. A sparkling ruby

sleeveless dress hugged her body like second skin, accentuating the fact

that she had pleasant, soft curves in basically all the places I didn't. The

slit on the left side went halfway up her toned, tan thigh. Light reflected off the healthy, glowing skin of her smooth, round shoulders. Her espresso hair was pulled into a sleek twist, tucked and held in place with a beautiful ruby-studded silver comb. Her makeup was subtle compared to mine—bronzey, contoured cheeks and smoky gray eyes—but certainly none of us 'ladies' were going to avoid the bright red lips, courtesy of Beelzebub.

She looked like a cross between a Golden Era Hollywood starlet and Jessica fucking Rabbit. I cleared my throat, averted my eyes and traced the grout between the tiles of the island.

"Yeah, well, don't underestimate my ability to start having a shitty day very early in the morning," I replied with an eye roll and exaggerated groan. "I'm adept."

"I'm starting to realize that," she laughed. Then she pulled one of the papers out of the stack and waved it with bravado. "Crepes?"

"Crepes?" I asked, looking up at her. My brow released the morning's furrow, allowing my eyes to widen. "Really? You know how to make crepes?"

"You like crepes?" she asked with a grin.

"Are there people who don't? Is that a thing?"

"I'm not sure," she giggled with a shrug of her perfect shoulders.

JESSICA BENOIST-YOUNG

"I think there are people who like crepes and people who don't realize they exist," I declared.

"Aright, what's your favorite filling, then?" she interrogated with a smirk, shifting toward me.

"Oh, putting me on the spot," I drawled dramatically. "I mean, I have many favorites, but I suppose if I had to choose *one*, it would be *dulce de leche*."

"*Mmm*," she hummed, closing her eyes and licking her lips. "*Dulce de leche*. Now you are speaking my language. Lucky for you, I happen to be an expert at making *dulce de leche*."

"Lucky for me," I echoed. "It will likely be the only luck I have all day."

Catalina slid the recipe to me to look at and pointed at a few items she wanted me to gather.

"Feel free to get it off your chest," she said, grabbing her apron from its hook and sliding it over her head. "Or feel free to toss around the mixing bowls. Just, you know, not the ones I need for these crepes," she added with a wink.

I laughed through my nose as I pulled my apron on, too, tying it behind my back, realizing with horror as I did that I had a large red ruffly bow sitting atop my ass. I groaned and yanked the red gloves off, casting them behind me without a shred of care where they landed. In the trash, I secretly hoped.

"Well, this cheap, slutty sexbot outfit doesn't help," I started, then the rest all came tumbling out in a rushed and frustrated word spillage. "But mostly it's the fact that everyone thinks I'm the Devil. I don't know why, other than I'm new and the weird shit on the island. And Didi—it's probably Didi! She's the one that originally wanted this stupid Burlesque shit, and she loves humiliating me. One of those Ds stands for Devil, I know it!"

"Slow down a minute," Catalina murmured. "Slow down."

I was so caught up in my rant, I didn't realize I had been haphazardly tossing the ingredients she'd asked me to get onto the counter top, causing a bag of flour to spill and throw a cloud of white dust into the air between us.

"First of all," she said as she calmly cleaned up the flour mess, then went about measuring her needed amount, "you have no reason to be humiliated. Secondly, I don't think you're the Devil."

"Yeah, I know," I muttered, grabbing the strawberries I'd gotten from the magic fridge and took them to the sink to wash. "Or, at least, you're reserving judgment."

"Oh. You heard that conversation…"

"Yes. I did. And if Todd and Company weren't all convinced last night, now they are extra convinced because I said I got a long list of names on my invite and nobody else did."

"Why would you need a list of the Devil's names if you are the Devil?" Catalina asked, cocking her head and scrunching her face.

"Fuck if I know," I replied with a shrug. "I guess it's a sign to them of my close ties to him, or something stupid. What did your invitation say?"

"Diablo," she answered without looking up from her task of cracking eggs for crepe batter.

"Oh, that makes sense," I remarked.

I brought the strawberries back to the island and started to slice away their leafy tops, letting them drop into a glass bowl once they'd been beheaded.

"Wait," I said, holding up my tiny paring knife, "so, it could be someone who speaks Spanish."

"I think most English-speaking people know Diablo, Michaela," Catalina chuckled.

"Todd speaks Spanish!" I declared like I'd just discovered a new planet.

"*Mina*, stop!" Catalina laughed, stopping her fervent whisking to look me straight in the eyes. "You want it to be Didi or Todd because you're mad at them."

Dropping my head in embarrassment, I sighed, "I know."

"Don't focus on that," she said. "Don't focus on who it might be. If your mind wants to fixate on something, fixate on the puzzle."

"The puzzle..." I echoed. "The puzzle."

"That is what I said," she responded, watching me with a tight forehead.

The song that had helped me figure out how I came to be on the ship popped into my head at the mention of 'puzzle'.

"Guess my name," I whispered.

"I know your name, I don't have to guess," Catalina muttered. Then, recognition hit her and she dropped her whisk into the batter, her eyes going wide as she looked up at me. "Oh!"

"The identity is the puzzle," I said excitedly. "He wants us to find out who he is."

Catalina's face lit up for a split second before falling in defeat.

"If he expects it to be unanimous, we will never agree," she grumbled, shaking her head. "Not this group. Look at how they're already pointing fingers everywhere."

"Well, in their defense, I did it, too," I sighed. "And it hasn't been *everywhere*. It's mostly been in one specific direction."

I pointed at my own face and tucked my lips to the side of my face.

"Do you care what they think?" Catalina asked.

"I don't want to," I answered. "But, if it's the difference between being stuck here and getting the hell out..."

"Good point," she conceded. "Though, I'd wager the best way for all of us to go into this is with limited emotions. Not paranoia or mistrust, but...safe distances and plenty of isolation."

Limited emotions. Safe distance. A strange disappointment pulled at the bottom of my chest.

"Sure," I agreed with a half-hearted nod. "Makes sense."

She appeared to be done with the batter, so I stooped down to survey the shelves under the island for the appropriate cookware for the crepes. When I stood back up, square griddle in hand, Catalina had moved closer and stood right in front of me.

"I didn't mean with you," she said softly.

My breath quickened and stomach churned. "Of course."

"I mean, we're still going to see each other in here, three times a day...every day."

I swallowed hard and handed her the griddle. "Yep."

Her fingers brushed the back of my hands as she took the pan from me, causing a ripple of prickled skin up my arm.

"Let's just get through this Burlesque Nightmare, and then we'll come up with a plan, alright? You and I."

Nodding, I echoed her in a distracted murmur. "You and I."

"*Bueno*," she smiled. "Now, let's *dulce* the fuck out of some *leche.*"

CHAPTER 14

BURLESQUE NIGHTMARE

I chose not to eat my delicious crepes in the presence of the people who suspected me of being the Devil, instead eating my breakfast in the kitchen, alone, since Catalina had gone out to sit with Lucian at the table. After devouring my breakfast, I retreated to my room and hid, telling myself I was 'keeping a safe distance', but really just knowing I couldn't be around any of them.

When we returned to the kitchen for lunch, my stomach sour with an eager anxiousness, it was completely emptied of food. Nothing in the magic Devil fridge. None of the pantry staples. Hardly a utensil in sight.

I tried to remain calm as I watched the panic seep into every corner of Catalina's face, her smoky eyes set square on the row of large steel pots on the island, each one adorned with a set of huge tongs straddling their rims.

She opened her mouth to say something, but nothing came out, and her eyes sought me for an answer with frenzied desperation. Jumping into action, I grabbed each pot, tilting it toward me to look inside, hoping wildly there was something in their metal depths—anything, a fucking box of cereal or a package of hot dogs. My stomach flipped so violently I thought I'd be sick when I saw what lie at the bottom of the last one.

Snatching the little red square out of the pot, I drew it out swiftly, eliciting a horrified gasp from Catalina on the opposite side of the island. I ripped open the envelope and read the note: "Everyone will be helping you prepare tonight's feast. *Catch* you later. Love, DD. P.S. Check the refrigerator again."

Catalina twitched in place then turned and rushed to the fridge, yanking it open with haste. She gasped again, just as horrified as the first time. *"Dios mio, no...no, por favor, no."*

"What—this doesn't sound good, what?" I rambled nervously as I rushed to her side.

The shelves were now filled to the brim with giant, wrapped, cream-colored blocks and sunny yellow footballs.

"Butter and lemons," I muttered.

"Butter and lemons," she echoed drearily. *"Catch."*

As I put the words together in my head, I heard a *clickety-clack* behind us. Slowly, in a terrified unison, we turned back to survey the island. Skittering across the shiny salmon tile, a scarlet-red crab happily snapped its giant front pincers as it approached us.

I screamed at the top of my lungs and grabbed onto Catalina, who had also taken to shrieking, for dear life. We clutched each other, jumping backward when the crab reached the edge of the counter nearest us.

"Oh my god! What do we do?!" I cried.

"I would say get up on the island, but he's on the damn island!" she blubbered.

"How many of these do you think he wants us to catch?" I whimpered.

The crab fell to the floor at our feet with a hard, plastic-like clunk, kicking off a second round of hysterics. This time, we did crawl up on the island, splitting to opposite sides of it to avoid the crustacean, then meeting back in the middle. With the four large pots, which I now realized were for boiling the crabs, and the two of us, there wasn't an inch of extra room.

"Wait," I said through shaky, hyperventilated breaths. "I have an idea."

I grabbed one of the pots and flipped it over, then scooted slowly and carefully to the edge of the counter top. Aiming the overturned pot over the crab, I lowered it as far toward the ground as I could before letting go. The pot hit the ground with a metallic clang, rocking from side to side. We watched with bated breath as it spun and shifted to the tune of a tinny whir, and didn't breathe until it settled completely over its intended captive.

"Oh, thank god," Catalina sighed.

"You do know how to cook these things, right?" I asked.

"Yes! I worked at a four-star seafood restaurant! But I didn't have to catch them myself! And they had those bands on their claws," she ranted breathlessly.

"Alright, well, I'll look around for some other ways to catch them...nets, or potato sacks or something," I muttered, sliding off the island carefully, not taking my eye off the pot that confined the crab. "You go tell the others—"

My sentence was interrupted by a shouted string of profanities from the lounge area.

"Too late," Catalina stated.

We dashed to the lounge, huffing and puffing when we arrived to find Bob up on a bar stool, and Todd cornered behind the bar, sweeping at a crab that tried to come near him with a broom.

"Crabs!" Todd yelled in a panic.

"Yeah, we know," I groaned.

"We have to catch them," Catalina said. "Everyone does. That's our dinner."

"Says who?" Todd rebutted.

"Says *him*," Catalina barked. "We got a note when we were getting ready to cook lunch."

"We've already trapped one in there," I added, scoping out the crab under Bob's bar stool, trying to figure out how I could catch it.

"Well, someone go get the twins!" Todd demanded, voice on the brink of hysteria.

"You go get them," Catalina snapped, glaring at him, the angles of her face and posture suggesting she did not want to be told what to do by him.

Todd returned with a glare of his own before conceding with a sigh and crawling up over the bar to escape the crab that blocked his way out. Once he had left the lounge in search of the resident fishermen, I turned back to Bob, who whimpered as the large crab underneath him curiously clapped his pincers around the legs of the stool, as if trying to figure out how to climb up.

"Do something!" he pleaded to me.

"Oh, you want *my* help?" I asked facetiously, a hand resting atop my abnormally generous cleavage. "What if I'm...*Lucifer*." I raised my eyebrows and grinned slyly.

"I don't think it's you, alright?" Bob said. "Everyone just thinks that because of the four days on the island thing, and since you're the newest. But, they forget that weird things have been going on for several months."

I stared at him in silence for several moments, contemplating his words. *Weird things had been happening for several months...*

"Give me your blazer," I said, holding out my arm.

He pulled the scarlet blazer off, revealing a white Hawaiian button shirt patterned with red palm fronds, and tossed it to me. Holding it open, like a net, I lunged at the crab, my heart pounding, and wrapped it up quickly in the blazer, tying it off as best I could with the sleeves.

"Where should we put it?" Catalina asked.

"The bar fridge," I answered.

"No! That's where the other one is!" she said, pointing behind the bar where Todd had been standing. I rushed to her side and looked. It was tapping the front of the bar fridge with its big front claw.

I growled in frustration as the living bundle squirmed in my arms.

Bob crawled carefully down from the bar stool. "Why don't we pick a room and shut them all in there until we can figure out some sort of net or cage?" he suggested.

The crab in the blazer wriggled and jerked and I clamped my arms around it tighter. "That's actually a really good idea."

"The kitchen office?" Catalina posed.

"Sure," I agreed with a quick nod before heading back to the kitchen with my catch. Catalina followed.

"Okay, so I'll just stand here...and...watch this other one, then!" Bob called after us, his voice nervous.

I tossed the blazer crab bag into the office while Catalina scooted the upturned pot with crab number one in, as well. Once both were in, I slammed the door with gusto.

"Jesus Christ," Catalina sighed, collapsing against the wall.

"What did he mean about weird things happening for several months?" I asked.

Catalina shrugged. "Beyond the normal weird stuff? I mean, it's all weird, Michaela."

"Yes, beyond the normal weird stuff—anything that it seems would indicate an extraordinary level of involvement from the Devil."

"Well, there was Monte Carlo Night," she answered with a shrug. "It was sort of like this Burlesque thing. We all woke up dressed in nice clothes and the dining room had transformed into a casino. We had to gamble until we had lost all of our chips, and it didn't end until *everyone* had lost all their chips—which, if I remember correctly, ended up being almost a whole twenty-four hours. Bob is really good at black jack. Took him forever to lose everything that he had won in the first few hours, when we all thought it was fun."

I bit my lip and squinted my eyes. "Why has everyone forgotten that?"

"No idea," she replied. "Probably because they're ready to jump to conclusions about you. Like I said, it's no time to be irrational and make judgments—"

"Whoever it is, they're trying to frame me," I cut in as the realization presented itself. "So, whoever keeps persisting in these reasons as to why it's me—"

"You're not listening to me at all," Catalina interrupted, laughing and shaking her head in disbelief, "are you?"

"—is probably the Devil," I finished my statement without acknowledging hers.

She peeled herself away from the wall and sauntered the few steps toward me. "You need to take your mind off this," she declared.

"Well, you would think running around catching giant crabs would do it," I chuckled.

"I'm serious," she said, her voice going soft and low. She took my bare shoulders in her smooth hands. The gulp my throat insisted upon, against my wishes, was embarrassingly audible. "You need to relax. You look like you're going to be sick."

She felt my forehead with the back of her hand, which I assumed was a maternal compulsion, and apparently I passed the test, shrugging and puckering her lips as she took it away.

"Anyway, Jeff and Jeric will figure out the crab situation, I'm sure," she said. "And no one is going to figure out this puzzle tonight—not with this Burlesque business going on, and *especially* not with everyone pointing fingers at every chance," she added in the tone of a lecture.

"Fine," I groaned. "I'll stop."

"I thought you already had," she smirked.

"I did, for awhile..."

I bit my lip and lowered my chin in mock embarrassment.

"Well, you've got one more on your side, anyway," Catalina sighed and smiled. "So the next time you feel like everyone thinks it's you and you're about to spiral down the drain of your own paranoia, remind yourself that you've got Bob."

"Bob," I giggled. "Fantastic."

"And me, of course," she added. "You have me."

"Better," I murmured.

We locked eyes, and her smile vanished slowly, her expression going serious, her gaze dissecting me.

"Catalina..." I whispered.

"Three more!" Jeff's voice boomed as he and his brother stomped triumphantly into the kitchen with a wriggling, lumpy sack made from a bed sheet, causing both of us to jump and break our connection.

"In the office," I stated with a directive jerk of my thumb toward it. They tossed their makeshift net in with the others.

"How many more are there?" Jeric asked, his green eyes wild with excitement.

I shrugged. "No clue. He didn't say."

"It's like an Easter Egg Hunt!" Jeff uttered in elation. "But with *seafood*!"

"I know!" Jeric replied as they turned to leave the kitchen and presumably finish their quest. "It's *so much fun!*"

Once all the crabs had been found and caught, almost entirely by the twins, besides my first two and with one assist from Vivienne, who had kicked one off the shuffleboard deck and into the pool, where it was easy for her to scoop out with the pool net once she was done with her game and aware of the situation.

All in all, there were eleven—one for each of us—which, given their impressive size, was more than we could ever hope to eat in one night. But, we cooked it all anyway. Tracie bustled into the kitchen a few minutes before five o'clock to inform us that the tables had all vanished from the dining room and reappeared around the stage in the lounge.

"Oh, great," Catalina grumbled. "Dinner theatre. With crab legs."

"Sounds like a real cruise," Tracie muttered meekly.

I laughed through my nose. Then a thought occurred to me. "Wait, what's the *show* going to be...?" I asked nervously.

"I hope not female striptease," Tracie sighed as she grabbed a tray of crab legs to carry to the lounge. "I don't know if Bob's heart could take it after all the crab business today."

Catalina and I exchanged an amused glance behind her back as she exited the kitchen, then we followed with the other trays, laden with cayenne-colored, steaming legs and pincers, each with a large bowl of butter sauce for dipping and lemon wedges for squeezing.

The lounge was dim and the tables adorned with red tablecloths and little glass votives, which, for their size, radiated an impressive amount of golden glow. A spotlight cast a blinding white light on the empty stage. Everyone looked at each other awkwardly, nervously, clearly awaiting whatever twist in the Devil's plot would occur next.

I placed my tray of crab legs on the table nearest the stage and noticed another red square, barely discernible from the tablecloth of the same color except for its black, block-lettered print.

HERB LANCASTER

EMCEE

I grabbed another one from the seat next to it and examined it, too.

TODD DRAKE

#2

"Guys, we have place cards, and...I think we're the performers," I said. "Herb's says he's the emcee, and Todd's has a number on it."

Catalina set her tray down on the next table over and snatched up one of the tiny red tents, reading it aloud: "Vivienne Bordeaux, number four."

"You think that's the order we perform in?" Todd asked, walking to me and taking his card from my grasp.

"Yes, I think she's right," Catalina said.

Herb jumped on stage and cleared his throat loudly into the microphone. "Ahem! I'm starving and I wanna get hammered drunk tonight, so let's get this show on the road—you know, where I used to live." He chuckled at his own joke, but everyone else seemed too nervous at the prospect of what their performance might entail to join him. "Get it? I lived on the street—never mind. Well, look here! The karaoke screen is telling me that our first performer, or should I say *act*, is the lovely couple that started it all—let's have a round of applause for Bob and Tracie Millstone!"

Herb clapped enthusiastically as he backed off the stage so they could come up. As soon as they were in the spotlight, he rushed to his seat and began devouring crab legs noisily. Todd sat slowly next to him and shrugged.

"It says something, Bob—I can't read it," Tracie mumbled, squinting at the karaoke screen in front of them.

"It says *Adam's Fifth Birthday*," Bob read. Then, the two exchanged a glance and broke into hysterics.

"Okay, okay everyone," Tracie giggled into the microphone, "give us two minutes to set up. Find your seats...and-and eat some crab!"

The rest of us milled around the tables, looking for our place cards and sitting when we found them. I was at a table with Catalina, Lucian, and Didi, and I was listed as the fifth act. Catalina flashed me her card.

Number three. And she looked terrified.

"You're a professor. You get up in front of people all the time," I whispered, trying to be encouraging. "You'll be fine."

"I'm going right after and actual performer, Michaela, and I also have no idea what the Devil is going to make to do—or what will happen to any of us if we refuse," she rambled back to me in an agitated rasp.

"Alright, well then my next word of encouragement is *drink*," I murmured. "Drink a lot."

She jumped from her seat and rushed away, returning in under a minute with a bottle of sparkling white and two glasses. "How are you not *nervous*?!" she snapped as she opened the wine and poured, her hands trembling.

I cocked my head at her and furrowed my brows. "Are you serious?"

"Oh, right," she said, looking over her shoulder at Lucian. "I forgot. You're a....*performer*, as well."

"Something like that," I muttered before taking a gulping swig of the wine.

Bob and Tracie finished setting up their act, and as soon as they said they were ready, comical music blared out over the sound system. Bob stood behind Tracie and put a black sheet over his head. She held up his red blazer, which I feared smelled of crab from being used as my net earlier, in front of her body and he slid his arms through.

In front of them they had set up a table with several items, including a glass of water, a cell phone, and a plate of crab legs, and much to everyone's amusement, they worked their way through the props with Tracie narrating and Bob acting as her hands, despite not being able to see. The funniest bit of their act, though, definitely occurred when he tried to crack the crab legs, dip them in butter, and feed them to Tracie, which resulted in hysterical giggles and a large mess.

We all applauded as they removed the blazer and Bob pulled off his head cover and they shared a bow. Herb hopped back up on the stage, butter trickling through his beard and crab still in his mouth, while Bob and Tracie cleaned up their table and props.

"On his impending North American tour, you can catch one of our next performer's shows for just around fifty dollars," Herb announced. "Or, as he likes to think of it, a gram of cocaine."

Again, Herb chortled at his joke, but all he got from his audience was strained, tense silence.

"Well, I hope you weren't planning on telling any jokes, Todd, because this crowd sucks," he grumbled. "Come on up, Mister Todd Hippie-middle-name Drake!"

Todd trudged onto the stage wearing his signature wily smirk.

"Hello, and good evening. Thanks for coming out tonight. I know there are a lot of other places you could be right now, so this means a lot."

I giggled softly, and I wasn't the only one. His eyes flickered to the karaoke screen briefly, and his stage persona completely took over.

"See, Herb? They can laugh. So maybe it's just you? Look, not everyone can be a professional. Speaking of which, you're all going to get to hear some of my tour set. My tour did not originally include crabs, but it probably would have by the end."

Definitely more laughter, and it noticeably fueled him, straightening his posture, sharpening his eyes, twisting his lips, and infusing character into his voice. Under the spotlight, mic in hand, laughter from the crowd, he suddenly oozed comedy from his entire body.

"So, I like to start off talking about my family. I have a niece. She's not quite a year old, and recently I was visiting my sister. My sister asked me if I wanted to help put the baby to sleep. I said sure. So we go into the baby's room, and I'm holding her and doing that weird bobbing, swaying thing that every human knows how to do as soon as there's a smaller creature in their arms, and she starts up some lullabies on her phone. Suddenly, these lullabies start to sound really familiar to me. And it's not because I remember them from my childhood—no, because this wasn't *Rock-a-bye, Baby*, or Twinkle Twinkle Fucking Star—it's because it was a song from much more recent memory. It was a lullaby version of *Panama* by Van Halen.

"So, I think, this is weird, but whatever. Next song comes on and it's *Beautiful Girls*!! A lullaby version of Van Halen's *Beautiful Girls*—I turn to my sister and say: 'Tonya, what the fuck is this'? She says 'it's the Van Halen lullaby album'. And she didn't just say it like I *should* know, she said it like I was a very stupid person for *not knowing*. I said, 'There's a whole album of Van Halen lullaby covers?' And she informed me that, yes, it was a whole album of Van Halen lullaby covers and that there were a lot of other albums for *different* rock artists so that parents could listen to their favorite rock songs and the baby could listen to a lullaby. I said: 'Tonya, if you can't stop listening to your favorite rock music for twenty minutes to put your baby to sleep, I think you should be a groupie and not a parent'."

The din of raucous laughter drowned out even the noisy cracking of crab legs and clinking of utensils.

"Needless to say, she didn't find that funny. And then she said the thing that everyone says: 'Well, you're not a parent. Wait until you're a parent and you have a baby, then you'll know'. Which makes sense. So, then I'm always thinking about what it would be like to have kids, and I had an epiphany—I'll never have kids. It has to be a nightmare. My sister, a smart, successful human being is so desperate for twenty minutes of *fucking Van Halen* by eight o'clock at night that she's willing to take it in the form of a *lullaby*!"

Tracie's howling and snorting stood out above the rest of our combined laughter, and next to me, Catalina covered her lips with her fingers and giggled.

"That's like going to buy some blow and the dealer handing you a pixie stick," he laughed. "It's just not the same! It's just not the same...so, that's how I know it's rough. It's some rough shit. But it gets better. They grow up, they start walking and talking. They say some hilarious shit, and that's probably the best—that's the peak—when they start their unintentional preschool comedy careers. I was just at a coffee shop the other day and the guy in front of me had his little daughter with him—she was maybe three years old—and he ordered his drink and pastry, and she ordered her drink and pastry. The barista looks at the little girl and says

'I'm so sorry, we are out of that muffin, sweetheart. Maybe you'd like a croissant?'. The little girl says 'What the *fuck* am I gonna do with a croissant, *Brenda*?! It doesn't even have chocolate chips in it!' Hey—at least she didn't just flop to the floor and throw a tantrum like the rest of the amateurs her age. The best part was that the barista's name was Charlotte," he chuckled. "I don't know where the fuck Brenda came from. I loved it."

His eyes flickered back down to the karaoke monitor, then he looked back out across the tables and his small, but highly entertained audience.

"I'm supposed to wrap it up, folks, so I will leave with you a bit of advice before I go. It's pretty simple really—don't get caught up in the obsession with labels. Everyone wants to know exactly what they are and they want to tell everyone else. Like, we never really grow out of that Scout phase of collecting badges, or patches, or whatever, right? You know? We don't wear them physically on a vest or a sash, but we wear them. It's an extension of tribe mentality—we want to tell everyone what we are in case they are, too! And then we can be friends!

"You know what we do have, though, to do a little self-labeling for others to see? Bumper stickers. Which, you know, is a weird time to try and tell people about yourself. 'I'm a dog lover! I have four kids! I love Star Wars!' Look, we are all driving right now and I am never going to meet you unless you are going to the Starbucks on Cahuenga Boulevard right now, so not to be rude, but I don't care.

"Bumper stickers. I read them and I just laugh—and there are these people who just want you to know everything about them so badly that their entire car is covered in them. It's like, you should also add a bumper sticker that says 'I can't see out my rear window'. 'Proud rear view obstructionist'. I hope that person finds a nice community of other people who think seeing out the back of their car is overrated. They can get together...have coffee, and deep discussions about how they obstruct their rear view. Within the Rear View Obstructionists community, we may have some subsets, even smaller tribes—even more labels!. We already acknowledged the Bumper Sticker Enthusiasts, there are also Large Dog Breed Owners, and Friends Who Always Help You Move! What about people who put Beanie Babies and bobble-heads all over their cars?! That's a good one. Interior Vehicular Decor Specialists. Man, if I were that obsessed with labels, I'd be an alcoholic...

"Thank you! You've been the best crowd I've had all year!"

He went through an exaggerated round of bows while we

applauded and whistled, and Herb bounced back on the stage.

"Hey, thanks for warming 'em up for me, kid," Herb teased, nudging Todd with his elbow. "Now I can start my good material. Okay, *don't cry*, our next act is brought to you by Argentina. Please welcome to the stage Catalina Sosa!"

Catalina gulped and shuddered next to me, then stood slowly and plodded like a reluctant child up to the stage. I watched as her eyes went wide with horror as she stared down at the karaoke screen.

She cleared her throat nervously then looked into the crowd. "Does anybody have a condom?"

CHAPTER 15

FINGERS AND CLAWS

Herb had hardly made it back to his seat when he let out a loud, facetious sigh. "I don't know how old it is, so I hope you don't need it to work," he barked, turning around to head back toward Catalina on the stage.

"We are still talking about the condom, right?" Todd razzed him playfully, earning him more laughs.

"Hey! Your gig is over!" Herb shot back with a grin visible under his whiskers. He slid a small square package out of his wallet and handed it to Catalina, who took it nervously with trembling fingers.

"And, uh...a crab claw, please?" she muttered into the mic.

I had one on my plate that had likely gone cold during Todd's act, so I scooped it up and took it to her, curious what in the world she was going to do with a crab claw and a condom.

"This is some kinky shit," Herb mumbled with enough volume for everyone to hear, and a few chuckled, which pleased him.

"Welcome to Health 101," Catalina said, her voice shaky. "Today, we will be discussing...sex."

Whistles, claps and chuckles popped up across the lounge, like we were fucking teenagers, and Catalina's face blushed to the same color as her dress.

"I will be outlining safety precautions for sexual intercourse to prevent unplanned pregnancies and the contraction of sexually transmitted diseases," she continued. "One of the most easily accessible and reliable forms of protection against both pregnancy and diseases is the condom."

She held up the little foil square and it glinted in the light.

"Oh, extra large?" she joked. "Really, Herb?"

Laughter rippled across the room.

"Suddenly everyone's a comedian, hm?" he barked.

The positive reaction from the audience seemed to settle Catalina's nerves. She grinned, and the flush slowly drained from her cheeks.

"Well, since I have a rather large unit here myself," she stated, holding up the crab claw in the other hand, "the overestimation should work out just fine."

Everyone laughed again, including Herb, who also shook is head in mock disapproval.

"You know, Herb, why don't you come up here," she said, waving him toward her with the crab claw. "Come on up."

Still shaking his head, he plodded onto the stage and stood next to her. She handed him the crab claw.

"Herb is going to help me demonstrate to the class how to properly put on a condom. Now, usually, when I taught Sex Education, we'd have a banana, but Herb is used to larger, aren't you, Herb?" she teased.

"You know it," he joked.

"One important thing about a condom's level of protection is the fit," she explained as she tore the package open and started to slide it over the crab claw. "You don't want it to be too large for its...*occupant* or it

loses effectiveness. Gentlemen, resist the urge to stroke your egos or

impress your dates with a box of extra extra large magnums."

A loud *SNAP!* sounded as the condom broke, splitting open violently

and eliciting chuckles from a few people.

"Well," Catalina laughed, "usually you won't be putting a condom on

a crab claw—"

"You don't know my kinks," Herb joked to the approval of the

audience.

"And I don't think I want to, Herb," Catalina retorted with a grin.

"Anyway, kids, condoms will break, which is why a secondary method of

birth control is recommended when trying to avoid pregnancy, as well as

regular STD testing. Any questions so far?"

"Yes, I have a question," Didi trilled, her fake sweet voice alerting me

that she was likely about to say something bitchy. "How do lesbians get

pregnant if they don't sleep with men?"

"Didi, don't be a bitch," Todd warned.

"No, Todd, it's fine," Catalina said, though the question clearly

miffed her, her lips pressing tight and her eyes narrowing. "I know she's

just trying to push my buttons. But, it is important to discuss sexuality as part of sex education, as intercourse between a male and female partner is not the only type of sex.

"Didi, to answer your question, even though I suspect it was tongue-in-cheek...I am bisexual. I conceived Lucian with a male partner, before I entered a long term relationship with a female partner...the relationship you all know about and that I'm sure you're referencing with your terminology."

I looked to my left, noticing that Lucian did not seem uncomfortable with the topic of sex or sexuality or his parentage at all. Nor did Catalina seem bothered about discussing it in front of him, on a stage under a spotlight, nonetheless. *Biology professors must give 'the talk' pretty early,* I thought.

"I'm bisexual," Herb stated with boisterous pride.

"That's great, Herb," Catalina replied. "I'm glad you feel comfortable with your sexuality, and that you shared it with us."

"No point in keeping it a secret. The disco era was a wild ride," he purred suggestively, garnering a round of titters. "Well, this has been fun, but the screen is saying your time is up, Miss Sosa. And, I think I have one more condom, probably purchased at a fine upstanding discotheque in the late seventies, if anyone was inspired to do some safe nasty by tonight's Health class."

A smattering of applause accompanied Catalina's exit from the stage and she sighed loudly as she plopped in her seat between me and Lucian.

"See, that wasn't so bad," I said, nudging her lightly with my elbow.

"I didn't expect to get something I was actually practiced in. My first teaching job in Argentina was at a secondary school teaching health."

My stomach boiled with dread. *Something she was practiced in...*

So far everyone had gotten something they had done before, something they were relatively good at. Bob and Tracie were parents and were used to entertaining their kids, Todd got to do his well rehearsed comedy act, which was his job. And Catalina had done her job, as well.

I wasn't good at anything that could be transferred into a performance...other than the one thing I sold my soul to not have to do ever again.

The Devil couldn't do that to me...he couldn't make me do that...could he? Pulse pounding in my ears, thoughts racing through my mind, I hadn't even noticed Vivienne take the stage until her sweet, crisp, bell of a voice sounded in the microphone.

"This says I should sing a song from my time in jazz clubs in Paris," she said, her French accent thick, making her voice even more pleasant and interesting. "So, I will sing to you my favorite."

Her, too! I thought in panic. She was a singer and her performance was singing.

"I am so fucked," I muttered.

Catalina looked at me briefly, but our attention shifted in unison to the beautiful, haunting notes Vivienne began to produce. I didn't understand a word of it, but I knew what it was about just from her voice, robust and aching, guttural and moving, fluctuating between pain and desire, strength and vulnerability. Goosebumps covered my bare arms and my fishnet-stockinged legs. Next to me, Catalina shivered, leading me to believe she was similarly affected.

We were all completely silent as Vivienne's song filled the lounge. I closed my eyes, letting the music of her voice soothe my panic. It was easy to picture her, youthful and vibrant, in a little French jazz cafe, full of berets and smoke.

Her tune ended and I didn't want to open my eyes, and not just because I knew I was next. The notes lingered and hummed in my ears, and I knew if I pulled myself from the hazy jazz club in my mind, they would vanish, too.

Herb's raspy voice pushed the sweet sounds out, though, and my eyes popped open as my terror instantly resumed upon hearing him say my name.

"No way anyone is gonna top that," Herb said. "But, come on up anyway, Mickey Martin!"

Slowly, I rose from my seat and journeyed onto the stage, everything blurred by the bright spotlight once I was in place in its beam.

I looked down at the blue karaoke screen, expecting for a little pixelated Devil to pop up and chant "Strip! Strip! Strip!" in a cartoon bubble. But, instead, an actual karaoke screen popped up.

'TONIGHT, TONIGHT, TONIGHT'

IN THE STYLE OF GENESIS

"Fuck, I'm singing?" I uttered in disbelief.

"Sucks to be you!" Herb bellowed in amusement.

I pulled the mic from the stand, a daunting task with my sweaty palms. I vaguely remembered the song. I wasn't a huge Genesis fan, and my favorite Phil Collins songs all came from animated films. But, when the words started popping up in white on the blue screen, and the eighties pop percussion thudded through the room, I remembered that it was the one that had the weird lyrics about a monkey.

As confidently as I could, even though I knew there was no comparing to Vivienne's vocals, and I had no earthly idea why I was singing, let alone singing this random fucking song, I sang.

The lyrics in the chorus started to sound a bit more familiar to me, like they were emerging from an old rusting vault in my brain at the sound of the electric guitar and signature Phil Collins drum beats.

I looked out across the tables as I hit one of the sustained notes with pretty damn good pitch and power. Catalina wore a wide smile, half encouragement and half surprise. Didi scowled. Vivienne seemed uninterested. The twins murmured to each other with half-empty mugs of beer held aloft. Tracie and Bob grinned politely and bounced to the beat. Herb bopped his head, eyes closed, playing a set of air drums with bravado. Next to him, Todd glared at me, his eyes like daggers, and he shifted uncomfortably in his seat.

When I reached the bridge, he shot straight out of his chair and stormed out of the lounge. The shred of confidence I had built with my decent performance vanished and was instantly replaced with anger. *What the fuck was his problem?*

"Todd?" Didi uttered, standing and making her way after him.

"No!" I snapped into the microphone. "He's got a problem with me, he can talk to *me*."

I replaced the mic in its stand and rushed after him, catching him in the hall where our rooms were located. Hearing my footfalls, he turned and looked over his shoulder.

"I don't want to talk to you," he grumbled, looking away,

"Well, too fucking bad," I spat, running up next to him. "What the fuck is your problem?"

He stopped in front of the door to his cabin and mumbled as he prepared to go in: "Right, like I believe you don't know exactly what the problem is."

I followed him into the room. "If I did, do you think I would have rushed after you to see what it was?"

He rounded on me and I took a step back as he jabbed a finger toward me.

"Drop the fucking act, okay?"

"Jesus, Todd! I thought maybe you were just mad at me for leaving you on the deck, but you *really* want to believe I'm the Devil!"

"Well, it does feel a lot like you are here just to fuck with me," he snarled.

"Don't act like you didn't like it," I snapped back.

He puffed a laugh through his nose and crossed his arms, a smirk pulling the corner of his lips. "God, you're just like her."

"Like who?"

"Didi."

"Excuse me?" I spat. "I am *nothing* like Didi. Okay? I wanted to help you, and I still do, but not if it means being the roadblock between you and her crazy bullshit."

"Oh, come on, Mickey—the only difference between the two of you is that she *had* to lure me in, and you didn't. You knew I was attracted to you from the moment I saw you. But you still toyed with me and used me —"

"What the fuck are you talking about, Todd?" I uttered in a rage. "Are you serious? You think I'm just sitting around plotting ways to screw with you and get you in bed? Like I don't have my own shit going on—like everything just revolves around you?! Even if I was the Devil, I'd at least spend my time equally fucking with everyone. I mean that's just fair," I added in a sarcastic tone.

"How did you know about that song then!?" he shouted, throwing his arms out. "Huh?"

"I don't know anything about that song, Todd. I hardly knew the song going in. What are you talking about? It just came up on the screen, so I sang it."

"That song is about struggling with cocaine addiction," he growled. "I used to sing it to myself every night after fucking Didi just to get a few lines. Feeling like shit—like the shittiest person—like how could this shit keep coming back and how could I keep doing the most desperate shit for it?!"

"Todd, I didn't know...I'm..."

"Sorry?" he choked on an ironic laugh. "Yeah, me too."

"It's not me, Todd," I said softly. "I know you don't trust me, and you're not going to believe me unless you want to, but it's not me and I don't want you to do anything that makes you feel like shit about yourself. I know how that feels."

He cocked his head and stepped toward me slowly. "No, no, see...I don't think you do. You may have felt shame, but I don't think you ever truly hated anything you were doing. You have power over people. You always have. And you know it. And you stayed where you were for however long you did because you knew it. And you did it because part of you liked it."

I wanted to slap him, but settled for clenching my fists and jaw.

He stepped in again and ran a finger down my arm. My spine went rigid and my skin prickled.

"With one come hither, I'd be wrapped around your finger, and you know it," he breathed. "It's all this cool, calculated act to make everyone want you. I take it back—you're *worse* than Didi, because you're better at the game than she is."

I *really* wanted to slap him. Eyes narrowed and hands on my hips, I curled my lip and angled my head.

"Tell me," I drawled tauntingly, "how long did you rehearse those poor, puppy dog eyes and that gallant, sacrificial baggie toss before coming to my room so you could take me to bed?"

He stared at me in shock and anger, and when his chin dropped sharply to his chest and he exhaled a pained wry laugh, I regretted my words.

"Todd—"

"Just get out," he muttered.

"I didn't mean it—"

"Yeah, I think you did. Please get out."

"Todd, I'm sorry!" I tried again.

"Mickey, just go back to your precious, little Cat, okay?" he snapped. "She seems to have her claws in deep."

I had been ready to turn and leave, but a fresh wave of ire filled my lungs. "Speaking of claws, how long did you wait to run back to Didi after I jumped overboard? Is that what all this is about? You went back to her and you did that cocaine and now you're in withdrawal, aren't you?"

"First of all, you wouldn't know anything about how I feel—"

"How long did you wait, Todd?" I repeated.

"I thought you were dead!" he shouted. "Okay? After a day, I thought you were dead. And if you weren't dead, I thought you were at least long gone. I was not handling that well on my own."

I sighed and shook my head, throwing my arms up in the air. "We had known each other a little over a week!"

"Well, that week was the most intimacy I've shared with anyone in years," he retorted, his voice on fire, "so I don't know what it meant to you, but it meant a hell of a lot to me."

My stomach flipped and I swallowed hard. A rim of glistening moisture outlined his eyes.

"This place is like a fucking prison," he continued, his voice dropping to a soft murmur. "I mean, fucking Christ, my life before this was a fucking prison! I was locked in a goddamned cage of ambition and addiction. Before you, I hadn't had sex, let alone an intimate conversation, with anyone while sober in ages." He paused briefly as his words stuck in the constriction of throat. "I don't know why I'm telling you this, you've made it clear you don't care."

"Todd, that's not true!" I argued, stepping in toward him.

He held up his hands, signaling me not to come any closer, and a visible shudder rippled through his body. "Can I just be alone for awhile?" he asked.

"Sure," I whispered, backing up slowly. When I reached the threshold of the door, and he hadn't said anything else, I turned and ambled toward my room a few doors down on the opposite side of the hall, hearing him shut his door behind me as I did.

Turning the handle and leaning in, my shoulder rammed into the cheap, sea green door to my cabin unexpectedly.

"What the fuck?" I mumbled to myself.

I jiggled the handle and it hardly moved, a spastic staccato of reluctant, unyielding metallic clinks and clacks filling the otherwise silent hallway.

"What the *fuck*?!" I repeated, this time louder.

"Is everything alright?" Catalina strode toward me, her face cautious and concerned.

"No," I groaned, "I'm locked out of my room. Todd fucking hates me. And I'm a terrible person."

When she was close enough, she grabbed my shoulder and turned me towards her.

"You're *not* a terrible person," she said. "You're a bit angry at times, but you are accepting, and supportive, and thoughtful. Things get heated and people are unkind. Unfortunately, it happens. That doesn't make you a bad person. It makes you human."

I sniffled against the sudden presence of moisture in the corners of my nostrils and eyes. "Okay, but what about my door?" I whimpered, changing the subject.

Her face pulled into a grimace. "It's probably because you didn't finish your performance," she muttered. "Your punishment, of sorts."

"God, this is a nightmare," I sighed. "I guess I'll just sleep on the sofa in the lounge."

The grimace stretched wider. "They're still going."

"Of course," I groaned. "Of course they are. Well, there has to be a roll-away cot or something on this bullshit ship, right?"

She shrugged. "Probably. I can help you look, I just need to stop by the lounge and tell Lucian."

"Good, I need a beer," I said. "Or some wine. No, a shot. Yeah...a shot and a beer and—*ooh!*—a glass of *champagne.*"

"Alright," Catalina laughed, a sound that made me smile despite my mood. "Commence Operation Booze and Bed."

CHAPTER 16

NAUGHTY KNOTS

When we got back to the lounge, Jeff and Jeric were on the stage,

bathed in the white beam of the spotlight, engaged in some sort of knot-

tying competition. I watched as I poured two glasses of champagne at the

bar.

Jeff called out the name of a knot: "Midshipman's hitch!"

Jeric went about trying to tie it as quickly as he could, while his twin brother counted backwards from twenty, which caused his brother to giggle and fumble in his task. When Jeff was done with his countdown, and Jeric had not completed tying his knot, the latter took a shot of dark amber liquor from a row laid out on a table behind them.

Slamming his empty shot glass on the table and handing his brother the rope, Jeric boomed: "Reef knot!"

And off Jeff went, Jeric counting in descending order, and everyone joined him this time. When Jeff failed his challenge, too, he took his shot to a raucous chorus of laughter and applause. He took a dramatic bow when he finished his liquor, a goofball grin emerging from the vignette of his rust-colored beard.

And they started again, and kept going, occasionally getting their assigned knots in the time frame, but mostly just falling into progressively drunken giggles, along with everyone viewing the game. Catalina and I drank our glasses of champagne, followed by seconds, watching from the bar. After twenty minutes, and a baker's dozen of shots between the two of them, Jeff and Jeric bellowed in unison: "Naughty Knots, folks!" and took their bows to a standing ovation.

The crowd moved slowly but surely toward the bar, which I stood behind, in a swarm.

"That was the last act," Catalina murmured. "Now they want to party."

"A round of beers!" Jeric exclaimed as the group approached. Catalina and I started gathering glasses and filling them from the tap.

"Where's Todd?" Didi asked, her lip curled in disgust to find Catalina and I behind the bar instead of him.

"He wants some time to himself," I said coolly, flashing her my iciest stare.

"We'll see about that," she remarked with haughty arrogance.

"I still owe you a slap in the face," I warned nonchalantly as I pulled a foamy ale. "Go anywhere near him tonight, and I promise you I will pay my debt. With *interest*. Cheers!" I handed her the beer I'd just poured with an exaggerated smile. A bearing of my fangs.

Catalina snorted next to me and Didi's eyes darted to her with contempt. She plopped herself down on a bar stool in a huff, then turned to Tracie and struck up a conversation like she hadn't just been put in her place in front of everyone.

During the next hour as fill-in bartenders, Catalina and I did almost as much drinking as we did serving, especially after Lucian went to bed on his own around ten. She had stood with him in the doorway, speaking in

Spanish in a hushed, maternal tone, then kissed him on top of the head before returning to her spot behind the bar and ceremoniously tugging her hair out of its chic twist. I had watched in something like a trance as it spilled onto her shoulders, adorned with ample, coiling waves courtesy of the updo, and the contours of her tresses shining in the light still made me stop and stare an hour later.

Just before midnight, the party started to disband, Tracie and Bob heading off first, followed by Vivienne once she had polished off her bottle of 1978 Hermitage Cabernet Sauvignon, then the twins offered to walk Didi to her room on the way to theirs, and finally Herb toting a freshly opened bottle of beer with him out of the lounge after he had regaled us with one of his discotheque adventures involving a dance competition against his unit commander from Vietnam.

Once they were all gone, back to their own rooms, we cleaned up the cans and bottles and glasses and napkins, scrubbing splashes and drips and splotches from the bar top, trying to leave it as clean as possible for Todd.

"Oh dear," Catalina muttered, tossing her dishtowel into the laundry bucket when she finished with it. "We never found you a cot."

"Oh, well, I suppose I can just sleep in the lounge now that everyone's gone," I replied with a shrug.

"No! No, we said we would find you a cot and we will!" she slurred, holding her finger in the air as if making a historic proclamation. "It will be like an adventure."

"Alright," I chuckled, throwing my towel in with the other.

We stumbled through the halls, giggling every time we rammed into each other or the wall in our drunken, off-kilter gaits. Past the cabins we tiptoed and staggered, muffling our laughter as best we could, until we reached the storage room. I half expected it to be locked, as well, but the handle clicked open easily. Catalina flipped on the light switch, instantly bathing the cramped square room in icy blue light, revealing an array of cleaning products, hardware, light bulbs and linens on metal shelves.

"Bingo!" Catalina exclaimed, rushing back to the far corner of the storage room. A folded cot on wheels stood upright, tucked against the wall. We rolled the cot in its upright, folded position out into the hallway.

"That was easy," I muttered.

"Wait, where are we going with this?" she asked, poking her head out to the side of the cot.

"Well, I was going to say the lounge, but I'd feel really ridiculous if we came and found this cot just to put it right next to the sofa I could have slept on," I murmured.

"No, you want to have a door, for privacy," she said, her face scrunched up in thought. "The kitchen office?"

"Um, the *crabs*?" I spat back.

"They're all gone," she said.

"You don't know that! Maybe one of them hid!" I argued.

"Well, with that logic, maybe we didn't catch all of them to begin with and they could be hiding all over the ship," she declared in a matter-of-fact but poorly enunciated observation.

"Oh my god! Why would you say that? I am going to have crab nightmares for weeks now!"

"Now do you want a door?" she teased.

"Yes!" I laughed.

Together we rolled the cot all the way to the kitchen office, having to carry it up the steps which was a struggle in our inebriated states. Finally, after dropping it once, knocking it over twice, and crashing it into numerous objects, we made it into the kitchen office with the damn thing.

Once it was positioned next to the desk, we both stood on one side of it. "Okay, how does it open?" I asked, scanning the metal frame for some sort of latch.

Catalina ran her hand along the top, which she could reach with her extra inch of height she had over me, and her taller high-heeled shoes. Suddenly, it sprung open like a jack-in-the-box, causing both of us to jump and shriek as it clattered and clanged loudly against the tile floor. We stared at each other for a shared moment of shock, then broke into hysterical laughter.

Staggering and unbalanced, she lurched forward in her giggling fit. As I attempted to steady her by grabbing her arms, she tried to stand erect too quickly and keeled back, her legs hitting the cot and sending us both plummeting downward. She landed on the cot and I landed on top of her, a series of thumps and titters and groans. Our eyes met as I hoisted myself off of her with one hand on either side of her torso, and her face suddenly filled with intent, the laughter gradually fizzling out.

In the haze of my drunkenness, everything happened so quickly. Her hands were on my face, then they were pulling it down to hers. Flames ripped through my chest and my arms turned to warm jelly as her lips touched mine. Inhibitions gone, her kiss turned more pressing, more ravenous, and her hands explored the bare portion of my back.

If I had been sober, a thousand thoughts would have been flooding my brain, but in the fuzz of those fiery moments, I didn't have any, other than the realization that I liked it...and wanted more.

I woke the next morning alone in the cot with a pounding in my head like my brain were part of a drum set. Phil Collins' drum set. As memories came trickling back to me slowly, I heard a crash in the kitchen, then a knock on the door. I begrudgingly crawled out of the sheets, still in my fucking burlesque outfit which had seriously irritated my skin during my sleep, and opened it.

The sight of Catalina sent a whoosh of feelings through me, and clicked several memories into place with as tangible a sensation as if someone had slapped me.

"Aspirin," she groaned, her dark hair in a messy braid and a fresh face of makeup that didn't quite hide the fatigue caused by our adventure the previous night. She wore jeans and a black button-up blouse, the front left open with a black camisole showing. "In the desk."

I walked around to the drawer-side and pulled open the top right one, seeing the aspirin nestled atop a container of paperclips. It rattled as I tossed it to her, and she opened it and eagerly downed her dose.

"Can't they just have cereal for once?" she grumbled.

I pulled a pill out of the bottle and popped it in my mouth and swallowed. "I'm fine with that."

"If there's one thing I can stand less than this fucking hangover, it would be Didi bitching," she said. "Or any of them bitching, for that matter."

She pulled the fridge door open.

"What is it?" I asked cautiously.

"Something easy, thank God," she sighed in relief. "Biscuits and gravy. Look, I've got this if you want to go try your room, maybe get changed?"

"What, you don't like my burlesque bunny get-up anymore?" I joked.

"I like everything you wear," she murmured with a quick jump of her brow and a brief smirk. "I just figured you'd be uncomfortable."

"I am very uncomfortable," I agreed emphatically.

"Then go change!" she urged. "Go! I have this under control."

"Okay!" I laughed as she shooed me from the kitchen with a smile. "I'm going!"

As I made the short trek to my cabin, I pondered the previous night's events. The thousand thoughts that hadn't hit me during were certainly popping up now.

What did this mean? Where was this coming from? I had never been with a woman before. I mean, a few kisses when dared in college, but I was usually drunk and didn't really remember wanting it to go further than that...but, I also didn't remember taking the time to think about it, either.

I had always found women attractive, although, I figured that was more a recognition of beauty. I also hadn't thought about that much either.

The door handle clicked easily, much to my relief. A folded pair of jeans and a gray t-shirt sat on the desk, and I stripped out of the annoying, irritating burlesque ensemble with haste, replacing it with the vastly more comfortable casual attire. Teal flip-flops lay on the chair, and I snatched them up with a happy sigh. "Thank God. Or, not God. Sorry. Thank you, Beelzebub."

I slid on the flip-flops, rejoicing in their minimalistic solace as compared to the heels I had been subjected to for the entirety of the day before, and headed back to the kitchen. A voice stopped me before I left the hallway, however.

"Hey," Todd said, and I turned around to find him positioned casually in the threshold of his cabin. "Do you have a minute?"

"Sure," I responded, walking back toward him. "Just a minute, though. I should get back to help finish up breakfast."

"I just wanted to apologize for my behavior last night," he murmured, tucking his chin, his expression self-conscious. Then, he shifted his face back up and looked me in the eyes. "I'm sorry. I was a dickhead."

"I was awful, too," I mumbled. "I'm sorry for what I said."

"You already apologized, though, and I didn't accept it. But, I do now," he said. "And, I was hoping we could talk—not now, I know you have breakfast duty—but, maybe before lunch duty? At the bar? I'm assuming I have a mess to clean up from last night," he added with a soft chuckle.

"Nah, we got it for you," I said. "You're all set."

"Thanks," he smiled. "So, do you think you'll swing by?"

His face looked earnest, his voice nervous. I remembered what he had said about the importance of our intimacy to him and, suddenly, my mind turned to a sloppy casserole—I couldn't handle the prospect of more questioning, more analyzing, more processing my feelings and the potential feelings of others.

JESSICA BENOIST-YOUNG

I could sit and wonder what he wanted to talk about all day but I'd never know unless I just talked to him. "Sure, of course," I answered with a nod.

"Thank you. Again," he said warmly. And, I'm sorry. Again."

He reached out and squeezed my hand before turning and disappearing back into his room and gently shutting the door.

Slowly, I spun on my heels and traversed the hallway.

"Look what you did," I grumbled under my breath. "You put me in some kind of silly love triangle! *Again*! This is all your fault. I'm blaming you. You can have your damn flip-flops back, asshole."

I kicked wildly until the rubber shoes flicked off my feet, hitting the wall with noisy slaps.

"Making me have all these *feelings*," I grumbled in disgust. "Such an asshole. God, this carpet is disgusting. I'm taking these back." I snatched the flip-flops from the floor and slid them back on, then pointed at the ceiling. "But I'm still pissed at you! A lot!"

Herb emerged from the room to my left and I jumped.

"Two things," he said, his voice groggy and eyes drooping, "your little tantrum in the hallway is interfering with my hangover sleep."

"Sorry," I muttered my apology reluctantly.

"Secondly," he stated with a yawn, "you were pointing the wrong way." He pointed downward, drew a little circle with his finger, then abruptly slammed the door.

I looked down at the nasty, worn down, puce-colored carpet with its cheesy, yellow and green pineapple trim. In lieu of repeating my frustrations to him, I stomped the floor with my foot as hard as I could.

"Mickey! Fucking Christ!" Herb's muffled voice bellowed from his room.

I scurried out of the hallway and up the stairs, back to the kitchen, and one arm of the Devil's little triangle...

CHAPTER 17

CAT AND MOUSE

Nervous around Catalina again, and since she wasn't mentioning anything about the night before, I stayed relatively uncommunicative through the rest of breakfast prep and cleanup. The awkward quiet could certainly be attributed to our hangovers—that's what I chose to believe regarding her relative silence, anyway, in an attempt not to spend the time over-analyzing it, on top of every thing else I was trying to process.

Thankfully, the greasy, carby biscuits and gravy went a long way to ease my headache and sour stomach, and gave me a bit more vigor than I had before. When cleanup was done, I checked the clock. Nine thirty. I slipped off my apron and hung it back on its hook.

"I'm gonna go," I muttered to Catalina, who was seated in the office, eyes closed and rubbing her temples. "Not feeling any better?"

"I have not drank that much in quite some time," she groaned. "I had forgotten how awful this is."

"Well, I can certainly take lead on lunch," I offered. "And I can grab you an espresso from the lounge, if you think that would help."

"Oh, thank you, Michaela, but I think the best course of action would be to try and get some more sleep," she sighed. "I just feel bad—I usually try to spend this time with Lucian. And since I was out late last night..."

A look of embarrassment took hold of her face as she trailed off awkwardly. I kept my lips pressed tight, unsure of what to say. It was obvious she didn't want to talk about what happened...and any possibility that she didn't remember was out the window—her strange change in tone and expression all but confirming she knew exactly what happened but didn't want to discuss anything about the night at all.

"Anyway, I'm sure I'll be fine," she said, snapping out of the momentary gawkiness abruptly, as if she were circuited through a switchboard that someone else controlled. "If you see him, just let him know I'll be napping here." She gestured to the cot that still lay open next to the desk.

"Sure," I replied with a quick nod. Then, I left the kitchen, headed for the bar....and the other point on this fucked up triangle I had gotten myself into.

When I arrived in the lounge, bee-lining for the bar, Todd had a smile on his face and a Bloody Mary waiting for me.

"Hair of the dog?" he grinned, sliding the drink toward me.

"Oh, I'm feeling much better after breakfast, and I'm not a big Bloody Mary fan," I refused the offer as politely as possible.

"Okay, well I also have a back up," he drawled playfully, then proffered a tall flute full of bubbling gold. "Mimosa?"

"There you've got me," I laughed, taking the drink from his offering hand. "It is physically impossible for me to turn down a mimosa before noon."

He laughed, taking the Bloody Mary for himself, tucking the straw between his lips, but never taking his eyes off of me as I sipped at the champagne concoction.

"So," I started clumsily, "what did you want to talk about?"

Clearing his throat and setting his drink down, his face turned serious.

"I think we can solve the puzzle together," he said.

"Oh." I was not expecting that to be the conversation topic. And, I had all but forgotten about it after the Burlesque debacle.

"Look, I don't think the puzzle is an escape room like Cat mentioned to me the other night," he explained. "I think that it's actually the identity of who the Devil is posing as."

"That's what I think, too," I said slowly, surprised he had come to the same conclusion. It was slightly suspicious to me, but in an effort to gain as much information as I could, I quashed the thought.

"Great minds think alike, huh?"

"I suppose they do."

We locked eyes during sips of our drinks, and he smirked.

"Anyway, I think I've ruled out a few people," he continued, breaking the gaze. "Or, I guess, I've ruled out one."

"Who is that?" I asked, cocking my head.

"You," he said, his eyes serious and intense.

"That's a quick turnaround from yesterday morning, and last night," I chuckled wryly. "I think you're just trying to get on my good side."

"No." He shook his head and grabbed my hand. "Things were going on—weird crazy shit like yesterday—long before you got here. In my anger at you for leaving, and my shock that you were okay, I ignored that. I just...I jumped to conclusions and treated you poorly. I am sorry. And you were right about Didi. All of it. Everything. I've been an idiot."

"You did a lot of thinking on your night off," I joked.

"I did," he replied with a laugh, pulling his hand away.

"Is Didi one of your...suspects?" I asked.

He raised his eyebrows and inhaled sharply. "Yeah. Big time. But, that also feels really obvious to me. I don't know—what do you think?"

"Well, I kind of put the whole thing aside yesterday," I answered. "Just, didn't want to jump to any conclusions, like you said, especially amongst the chaos of the Burlesque business."

He tilted his head at me and squinted his eyes in thought.

"When you accused Didi in the hallway yesterday morning, did you think the puzzle was the identity yet?" he asked.

"No, I think...I think I put it together right after that," I answered, the sequence of events of the prior day fuzzy in my head since everything happened in chaotic, rapid-fire succession.

"So, you realized it might be the identity that we have to solve, and *then* you decided to drop it for the day?" he interrogated, folding his arms in front of his chest.

"Yeah, I guess so," I said with a shrug.

"That was your idea?" He raised his brows at me in question.

"Yeah—or, I mean..."

I trailed off. I knew what he was getting at. Catalina had persuaded me to ignore the identity puzzle.

"So, you said 'the puzzle is the identity', and how long until she told you to disregard it?" he inquired.

"Todd, stop, okay?" I snapped. "I get it."

"How long, Mickey?" he pressed.

"Not long, alright? Is that what you want to hear?"

"Not what I *want* to hear, no, but it's helpful information, Mickey— everything that happens is going to be. We need to pay attention to everything everyone says and does if we want to get out of here."

"Y'know what? I'm not going to *partner* up with you if this is just going to turn into some 'turn me against Catalina' bullshit," I said.

"I'm not trying to turn you against anyone," he argued. "But you have to admit it's a little suspicious."

"Everything is suspicious when you analyze it like this, Todd!" I barked at him. "That was her whole point in what she said to me—we could literally find reasons for it to be anyone if we look at it like this!"

"And if we don't look at it like this, we will miss important things," he rebutted, his volume staying steady, his voice remaining calm and matter-of-fact.

"You think this is important? You think her telling me not to be paranoid and jump to conclusions is some huge hint?"

"No, I think it sounds like logical advice. It's the timing of it that concerns me."

I sighed and shook my head. "I don't want to be part of some...some witch hunt, Todd."

"So it's fine when the witch hunt target is someone you don't like, but not when it's someone you do," he stated.

An agitated groan rumbled in my throat as I buried my head in my hands. "I can't believe you asked me to meet you here just to spout some jealous crap—"

"I'm not—Mickey!—I'm not jealous, I'm worried," he insisted. "She's manipulating you! You can't see it, but she is!"

Hot anger steamed in my chest. Somehow I stayed in my seat despite wanting to get up and storm off in a rage.

"Look, the fact that you're obviously angry with me for making observations about her behavior just goes to prove my point."

I closed my eyes and exhaled slowly through my lips, as if trying to soothe some physical pain.

He was right. Even if she weren't intentionally manipulating me, I was, at the very least, blind when it came to Catalina of my own accord.

"Don't you think it's weird that she's been so caring, so forward, *after* you got back from the island? After you realized there was a puzzle?" Todd questioned rhetorically.

"If it's her then she would have been the snake in the garden who told me about it!" I pointed out. "Why would the Devil tell me about the puzzle and then try to distract me from it?"

"To fuck with you! To toy with you, Mickey!" he uttered, throwing his hands in the air. "Don't you get it? This is a game to him—all of it! You're the mouse, he's the cat."

Cat. My gut churned uncomfortably and my throat went tight.

"Look," he said, sighing softly and taking my hand in his again, "I'm not saying it's her. It could be anyone. Just...just pay attention, I guess, is all I'm saying. Okay?"

His thumb stroked the sensitive skin of the back of my hand and goosebumps prickled my arm at the sensation. "Okay," I agreed, nodding slowly but staring at the union of our hands.

He pulled away slowly. "Sorry," he murmured, sounding self-conscious.

"No, it's...it's alright," I assured him.

"Please, Mickey, don't take pity on me," he whispered.

"I'm not."

"You don't want to get mixed up or stuck in the middle of things, or whatever. I get it."

"Jeez, you make me sound heartless," I groaned. "It's not like I flat out don't care about people, Todd. I just...this whole selling my soul to the Devil thing is stressful enough without getting entangled with everyone here. And, I mean, don't you want to go home? We're not going to see each other after this, so why would I do that to myself? To you?"

"What if we don't?" he asked, propping his elbows on the bar top and leaning in slowly. "What if we are stuck here, for some unfathomably long time? At what point will you acknowledge your feelings? At what point will you feel okay getting involved?"

"I'm already involved, Todd," I said. "That's just it. I already am. In just over two weeks I have a huge mess of feelings and drama on my hands. If we are here for any longer, just imagine the complicated web of shit I'll end up weaving."

"It's not like you did it all on your own, Mickey," he chuckled. "Other people have free will, too. Other people make decisions and contribute their shit. You're being too hard on yourself."

"I appreciate your words of support, but I'm not a new passenger on the 'complete and utter fuck-up' train," I sighed, following my statement with an enthusiastic drain of the last ounce of mimosa.

"Babe," Todd shook his head and smirked, "you're talking to the conductor. Another?" He took my empty champagne flute.

"No, thank you," I said. "I think I'm gonna go wash my face and lay down for a few before lunch prep."

"You feelin' okay?" he asked.

"Yeah, I'm fine, I just...have a lot on my mind," I answered.

"Understandable," he replied. "Look, I don't want to overwhelm you, so go rest. But, y'know, maybe we can meet after lunch, and we can touch base. I'm going to keep an eye on Didi, you can tell me if anything happens with Cat, or if anyone else does anything weird, we can talk about that."

"Sure," I agreed. I didn't see why not, especially if Catalina was going to continue to ignore me and the topic of last night. "Here?"

"Usually people play games in the lounge after lunch," he stated. "My room?"

I hesitated slightly, but agreed. "Okay."

"Okay," he said softly, his eyes searching me, his expression expectant, waiting for me to say something else. He must have picked up on my hesitance. When I didn't say anything else, he inhaled slowly, then smiled. "Okay, go lay down. I know how exhausting it is to stand behind this bar all night."

I stood from the stool, feeling like things were unfinished, but gave him a short wave and headed to my room anyway. When I reached my cabin, I splashed my face with cool water and patted it dry, then collapsed in a tired, overwhelmed, confused heap on the bed.

No sooner had my face buried in the pillow then I was thrown out of the bed, hitting the floor with a thud, as the ship lurched violently, rumbling as it dragged away from the beach.

I leaped to my feet and launched myself toward the porthole, shoving my face against the glass as I watched in part-terror and part-intrigue as, for the first time since I arrived, the view from it changed. Slowly but surely, the beach disappeared, and the ship fell into a subtle rock and sway in the sea's rhythmic wake.

A glint caught my eye and my vision shifted immediately up toward the thin layer of gray linen clouds, peering at something bright that broke through them—small, looking like a diamond under a lace doily. A diamond in the sky...it was a star. Except it wasn't really a star. It was Venus, looking like a star in the morning, as it did.

Venus, the Morning Star. *Lucifer*. And the little extra shine was a signal.

He was gloating.

CHAPTER 18

CONFESSIONAL

I rushed out of my room, nearly ramming into Herb near the

stairs. He held his arms out to the side to balance himself.

"Damn, am I still drunk, or are we moving?" he yelled after me as I

bounded past him up the stairs.

"We're moving!" I called back, loudly enough for him to hear me without me having to turn to look over my shoulder.

"Well, fuck me sideways!" I heard him holler.

I poked my head into the lounge, the room I had just left minutes before, and saw the twins crowded around the bar. A sporadic tinkling of glass sounded from behind it.

"There are several extra brooms in the storage room," came Todd's voice. "And I might need a vacuum for the small stuff. And a mop."

Jeff and Jeric nodded and left, and Todd stood up with a dustpan full of glass shards.

"Oh, hello," he said with a grin. "Long time no see. I take it you had a nice, long rest."

"Are you okay?" I asked, ignoring his joke.

"Yeah, fine," he answered, shrugging his shoulders, then dumping the glass in the trash can behind the bar. "Just a few broken glasses. Or twelve. And all the vodka."

"All the vodka?!" I echoed in shock. "Shit, Herb is gonna be so pissed."

"Herb?" Todd spat. "What about Didi? If you think she's bad now, that's *with* a regular infusion of martinis."

"We have to get out of here," I insisted.

"Yep," he replied with an emphatic nod.

He dropped back down to a crouch and carefully picked up the pieces that were large enough for him to grasp without cutting himself. "Look, Jeff and Jeric will be back any minute with a vacuum and mop to help me clean up this mess. If you need to go check on the kitchen, or anything."

"Right," I muttered. "Yes, I-I probably should. Make sure nothing's broken."

He looked up at me from his cleanup effort. "After lunch?"

I nodded. "Yes."

A wide smile claimed much of the surface of his face. "Okay. After lunch."

Turning slowly, I made my way to the kitchen, an onslaught of nerves attacking me the nearer to Catalina I drew. My conversation with Todd had made me slightly suspicious, but heavily guilty. I felt dirty, like his words against her had been written on me with permanent marker. Like I carried a stench of betrayal, whether or not that was what I had actually done.

I expected to see Catalina out in the kitchen, cleaning up some mess of pots and broken dishes from the sudden pitch out to sea, But, while there was a bit of a mess scattered around the floor, she was nowhere in sight. Slowly and quietly, I turned the knob on the door to the office and peeked my head in. She was still in the bed, rolled like a burrito in the pastel pink sheet, a pillow covering her head.

Mildly confused as to how she could have slept through the same careen of the cruise ship that threw me from my bed, I decided to let her sleep if that was how badly she apparently needed it. I had mentioned I would take the lead on lunch, anyway, so I supposed I should follow through and let her rest until she felt better.

Maybe she knew it was coming... I thought. *Maybe that's why it didn't wake her—she did it.* I shook my head, as if to physically shake the thoughts from it, making a note to mention it later so I wouldn't dwell on it or let paranoia take the thought and run with it now.

The fridge was filled with familiar ingredients. Familiar to me, specifically. Tomatoes, garlic, parmigiana, pepperoni, sausage, green peppers, onions, olives, pineapple, Canadian bacon...blocks and blocks of mozzarella.

So, the Devil was listening when I said I'd handle lunch, and chose to give me the thing I was most practiced in preparing. Making another mental note to share that information with Todd, I pulled out the refrigerated ingredients out and set them on the kitchen island, then stooped down to the shelves beneath to get flour for the dough. Just as I started to measure and mix, a loud stomping approached the kitchen.

Didi stormed in, Tracie following her, a smug look on the former's face and a fearful one on the latter's.

"What do you want?" I asked.

"I assume you are familiar with the luau menu?" Didi said, her pursed mauve lips curled in arrogant victory.

"We just had a fucking party—literally last night," was my rebuttal as I began to knead the dough in the mixing bowl.

"Well, apparently somebody felt bad that I didn't get to have *my* party that *I* planned, and tonight we're doing mine," she explained with her nose in the air. She thrust a grass skirt in my general direction. "All the luau supplies were in my room after breakfast."

"I'm not roasting a pig," I declared in my most definite voice. "Even if you wanted me to, there isn't enough time."

Didi sighed. "Well, you would know if you had attended the meeting instead of jumping ship in your panties, but we decided not to do a pig roast again."

"Then what do you want? I have to work with whatever he gives me," I pointed out. "It's not like I can just make whatever you want on a whim."

"Oh, trust me...he always gives me what I want for my parties," Didi said, raising her eyebrows at me. Alarms of suspicion blared in my head as I stared her down. *Another note for Todd,* I thought. "And we decided on Hawaiian pizza."

"Fuck," I muttered under my breath. "Looks like your pal Satan did you a solid again, *Didi,*" I snarled, pummeling the ball of dough with my fist and giving her a look that indicated I would love to do the same to her.

"Perfect!" she squealed in delight. "So, late lunch slash early dinner so we will have plenty of time for activities afterward."

"Jesus Christ, what *activities*?" I groaned.

"Hula dancing, maybe some water polo in the pool—oh, and a limbo contest!" she listed excitedly.

"The limbo in Limbo," I laughed, rolling my eyes. "How charming."

"Anyway, I don't want the pizzas until four," she ordered. "And in the meantime, you could make some chips and salsa or something. Maybe some of those cute little ham and cheese pinwheels. Bring them to the deck as soon as they're ready."

She flashed a fake smile at me then spun on her heels and left without another word, Tracie following her with the bundle of grass skirts.

"Maybe you could fucking say please, you snotty—"

"What was that about?" Catalina mumbled through a yawn as she emerged from the office.

"Apparently, it's Luau Day!" I answered with phony enthusiasm.

"We just had a party last night," she grumbled.

"That's what I said," I told her. "Speaking of which, how are you feeling?"

"Not great," she replied, laying her torso down on the island, her cheek against the tile as she looked up at me. "I jolted out of my nap a bit ago and since then everything has felt like it's spinning. Or swaying...like I'm drunk again. I hate this."

A giggle caught in my throat. "It's not you, Catalina. The ship is moving."

"What?" She shot upright.

"Yeah, pulled away from the beach and started moving."

"Oh, shit," she muttered.

"And now it's Luau Day," I sighed. "And she wants the pizzas at four. I'm going to pre-make the crusts. It will make the prep easier later."

"Good idea."

A shroud of tense silence slipped over us and I tried to ignore how it pressed on my chest and clung to my shoulders. I focused on spreading flour on the island and rolling my dough out in a large, thin circle. But, impulse won out, eventually, and I took a deep breath before launching into what I was certain was a huge mistake.

"So, do you remember last night? Or do you just not want to talk about it because it was a mistake? Or did you hate it? Did I suck? I mean, I haven't *been* with a woman before so I probably sucked, but you could just tell me—"

"Michaela! Michaela, no! Stop," she interrupted. "You didn't suck. And I do remember."

"Then why didn't you say anything all morning?" I asked, looking up from my pizza crust prep to meet her eyes.

"You didn't say anything either, Michaela," she said softly. "I was embarrassed, I suppose."

"Embarrassed about what?" I asked.

"That maybe you did it and you realized that it wasn't for you," she admitted. Her brown eyes were dewy with doubt.

I sighed, a swell of emotion lodging itself in my throat as soon as I went to speak. "I think that it is for me," I stated in a tight voice. "I-I don't really know, I guess."

"Well," Catalina murmured, "a pretty decent indicator is if you feel like you want to do it again. Do you?"

I bit my lip and nodded. She smiled in return, and nodded along with me.

"Alright. Well, that's a start," she whispered. She came around the island and grabbed my hand. "Look, I've been doing this for awhile, even came out to my intensely Catholic family when I was about your age, so...just know I'm here, if you have questions, or anything you want to talk about."

"How did you know?" I asked. "I mean, when did you *know*?"

"Part of me always knew, I think, but in my life, in Argentina, in a Catholic family and school, it was never an option for me, so I rarely acknowledged it," she explained, her face tight as she discussed her past. "But, I met Sofia after Lucian's father dumped me, rather abruptly, when Lucian was only a few months old. He was the chef, at the restaurant I had worked at for years, and...well, let's just say I found out the hard way that the restaurant meant more to him than his child, or myself.

"I met Sofia at my new job, and honestly, for awhile, I thought I was only considering a relationship with her, only enjoying it, because things with Pablo ended so horribly. I thought maybe I was just soured on men from the whole thing, but, as things went on and we continued spending time together and seeing each other, I knew that wasn't the case," she explained.

"What happened?" I questioned.

"Oh, nothing dramatic," she sighed. "We were together for seven years, and she wanted to move to Los Angeles and start a cosmetics company, and I wanted to stay at NYU and get married and maybe adopt together."

"I'm sorry," I muttered.

"It was three years ago," Catalina said. "Nothing to be sorry about. Lucian was diagnosed with his tumor and that was the final straw for her—her sign to move on, I suppose. I am glad Sofia left when she did. I wouldn't want her staying out of guilt. And I wouldn't want someone who didn't really want to be there for us by our sides. Anyway, I've completely derailed the conversation."

"No," I said, "I like getting to know more about you. I don't mind."

She smiled at me and grabbed one of the balls of dough that I had left to raise a bit in the bowl, then started to roll it out on the flour-covered tile next to me, our elbows brushing against each other as we worked. After we had finished four crusts, baking them each slightly in the oven then letting them cool and covering them with clean towels, we moved on to Didi's appetizer requests. Using the pizza toppings from the fridge, we scrounged together a makeshift pineapple salsa, and Catalina made flour tortillas, then fried some of them for chips and used the rest to make some pepperoni and mozzarella pinwheels.

We put the appetizers on trays and took them out to the deck. Clouds still clung tightly to the sky, blanketing the sun with their gray wool.

"Not really luau weather, huh, Didi?" I teased as I set my tray on a table she had decorated with a pineapple tablecloth and little paper palm trees.

"Oh, can it, Mickey Mouse," she snapped, not looking at me as she fussed with crepe paper along the railings.

Catalina trapped a chuckle in her nose and we exchanged smirks in our peripherals. She put her tray next to mine and we turned to head back to the kitchen to clean up.

"If you see Todd, tell him I need a pitcher of *Sex* on the Beach," Didi called after me. I froze and looked back at her, her lip curled into a taunting smirk.

"Sounds like something you'd rather tell him yourself, Didi," I said.

She shrugged and turned away from her decorating. "If you insist," she giggled, her jaunty steps toward the inside of the ship bouncing her large, prominent breasts.

I reached out and grabbed her arm as she made to pass me. "Don't fuck with him," I snarled in my throat.

"He's not *yours*, Mousey," Didi trilled.

"That's not what I meant," I growled. "If you *have* anything, keep it to your fucking self. He's trying, and if you care about him at all, you'll stop this little game you're playing."

Didi's swallowed hard and her face dropped slightly. Then, like the flip of a switch, it went right back to its default state of haughty, cold arrogance. She ripped her arm away from my grasp and stomped away without response.

I released a languid, aggravated exhale.

"Let's go cleanup the current mess," I groaned. "We have like six pounds of mozzarella to shred."

As we made our way back inside to the kitchen, Catalina put her hand on my shoulder and spoke in my ear. "You don't have to clean up all the messes, you know. His problem is *not* your problem."

I stopped abruptly and turned to face her, my ribs clamping down on my lungs, my breath hot as I huffed through my nose.

"You've tried, and you've been a good friend to him—better than any of us before you got here, apparently," she continued. "I mean, we all knew about it, but he didn't tell any of us he wanted to...stop."

"That's exactly why it *is* my problem!" I argued, my voice breaking in exasperation.

"No, it's not, Michaela," she rebutted, grabbing my elbows and squeezing them gently. "You *feel* like it's your responsibility, but in the end, it's his. It always has been, and he may need support, but, you're not always going to be around for him. You can't be the only thing that keeps him sober."

"God, is this how you're going to feel about me at some point?" I snapped.

"What?" she pulled back and tilted her head in confusion.

"I mean, my sexuality isn't your *problem* even though I opened up to you about it, and you're the person who made me realize it," I spat, my face flaming.

Her jaw dropped in offense. "That—this is not even the same thing, not even close," she sputtered.

"Isn't it?" I retorted, on the verge of tears. "Is that why you were quiet about it until I forced you to talk to me? God, I don't want to be anyone's *responsibility* if they're going to treat caring about others so callously."

Without giving her a chance to reply, I turned to leave her in the hallway.

"Hey!" she barked, rushing to catch up with me, grabbing me by the waist when she did and spinning me around. She was much stronger than I expected, and I gasped when she forced me against the wall. She leaned into me and put her lips to my ear lobe. "You *are* a problem for me. You are a *big* problem," she purred, "because I can't think about anything else since the moment you opened your door."

I couldn't breathe, my shallow attempts at it proving futile against the bonfire in my chest, which had started as anger and melted into desire.

"And I don't see you as an obligation because I had a role in your awakening," she continued. "But, I may or may not choose to find some responsibility in that. Certain areas of that."

"Like what?" I whispered breathlessly.

She looked me in the eyes and tilted her head slightly as she seemed to be searching my face for a word. She smirked when she thought of it.

"Fulfillment." In her accent, in her deep voice, and an accompanying seductive tone, the word that I used to associate with Amazon Prime suddenly became the sexiest thing I'd ever heard.

Her lips met mine and all the air left my lungs as if she had sucked it out herself. With a broken inhale, I tried to regain what I had lost, but when her lips traveled down my neck and traced along my collarbone, it vanished again.

She smirked and grabbed my hand and led me out of the hall and toward the kitchen, but I knew it wasn't to start our chores. We walked right past the mess of flour on the island and into the kitchen office, where the cot remained, almost like it knew we'd be back...

CHAPTER 19

EVERYBODY DANCE

An alarm on my phone signaled that it was time to emerge from the office and prepare Didi's stupid pizzas. As I watched Catalina slip on her scarlet apron reluctantly, a brief flash of hot nerves sizzled and seared across my skin—I was *supposed* to be careful, be observing, not getting more tangled up with her. What if it was her? What if she were the Devil?

Had I just slept with the Devil? *Twice in less than twenty four hours?*

I took a deep breath as I started the cleanup that we hadn't gotten to before.

"You okay?" she asked, pulling her dark locks back into a sloppy bun.

"Yeah, I just...don't want to go to this party," I said, which wasn't a complete lie.

"Tell me about it," she groaned. "But, hey! At least I get to finally try some of your specialty, right?"

"I promise you, it isn't that special," I laughed.

"I'm sure it will be better than if I attempted to make pizza," she countered. "Though I do have a request."

"Shoot," I replied.

"Could you do some that aren't Hawaiian?" she proposed. "I know Didi might flip because it ruins her theme, but some people don't like pineapple on pizza."

"Hey, if it'll antagonize Didi, I'm on board," I chuckled, pulling a block of mozzarella out of the refrigerator, preparing to undertake the task of shredding it. "But, since *you* brought it up as a *request*, I'm guessing you don't approve?"

"Of pineapple on pizza?" she chortled with a hand above her breasts. "God, no! It's a sin."

I dropped the block of mozzarella and it hit the floor with a spongy thud. We had called our pineapple pizza at Mitch's 'The Cardinal Sin'. *Did she know...?*

"Are you *sure* you're alright?" she asked again, her face screwed up in concern.

I ignored her, too many thoughts popping up in my head. She had been the first to come see me, practically reading my mind when she did. And knowing my full first name when I hadn't told anyone? Maybe the story of looking through my phone was a convenient cover.

Suddenly, I lurched forward, steadying myself against the cool tile of the island. *It couldn't be her...*

"Michaela," she said, "you are freaking me out."

I gasped for breath, clutching at my own neck. *It couldn't be her*, I thought, over and over again. It couldn't be her because...a fuzzy, wordless thought burrowed tangibly into my brain, causing me to wince and rub at my temples. *It couldn't be her...*

My breath came in hyperventilated pants and I faltered again. She lunged toward me to steady me, but I darted away, heading for the deck. My legs burned, my chest burned, my throat burned, and my eyes burned as I dashed through the dining room to the glass doors out to the deck where the luau party was in full swing, the others grooving to Elvis Presley and chit-chatting over bottled beers with hula dancers on them.

I panted for several seconds, trying to regain enough breath to say what I needed to say. Catalina rushed up behind me.

"What the hell is going on?" she asked, breathless from her sprint, as well.

"I know who it is," I uttered feebly through shallow breath.

"Oh, for God's sake, not this again," Didi complained, rolling her eyes.

Everyone's eyes were on me. They held their drinks aloft with bated breath, waiting for me to speak.

"Oh, you're not all serious with this right now, are you?" Didi spat. "She's just going to say it's me, and everyone will argue, and we'll waste all our time and the pizza will be late and this awesome luau will be ruined!"

"Didi, we're on a busted up, old-as-shit cruise to nowhere and Satan himself plays with us like dress up dolls!" Herb barked. "Your party, when put into those parameters: not that awesome."

She coughed in shock, sounding a bit like a cat succeeding at expelling a hairball. All eyes shifted to her briefly, but came back to me as I finally regained control of my breathing.

"We all have one thing in common, right?" I asked. "How we got here. How did you get here, Tracie? And Bob?"

"We were on a date for our anniversary and I said 'I would sell my soul to the Devil himself to go on a nice long cruise with you, honey'," Tracie answered.

"And I said 'Me, too, honey. Me too'," Bob said.

"God, that's really sweet," I laughed, but I quickly recovered my composure, whipping my index finger at the twins.

"Jeff, Jeric?"

"We were in a really bad storm in the Pacific," Jeff said.

"We were going to die, and our crew, too," Jeric chimed in.

"I heard Jeric mutter something about selling his soul to live through the storm, with all our crew safe and a net full of tuna, and I grabbed his hand and repeated it," Jeff recounted, nodding at his brother.

"Our daring tale of survival got us some notice from a few cable stations for reality shows," Jeric murmured fondly. "The day we signed our Animal Planet contract was the day before ended up here."

"I think everyone is quite familiar with what I sold my soul for," Herb boasted with pride.

"Mousey, do you have a point to all this?" Didi snapped. "Or can we please just enjoy ourselves?"

"Didi," I said slowly. Ignoring her remark, I pointed at her.

She swallowed and cleared her throat. "I...my husband was having an affair," she admitted, tucking her chin in shame. "Actually his third. Um, but anyway, I said I would trade my soul if he'd never cheat on me again."

A tear rolled down her prominent, taut cheek.

"He stopped...and then he divorced me two months later," she cried, her lips quivering.

I couldn't believe that I actually felt a pit of sympathy for Didi growing in my stomach.

"Wait, I thought, everyone's life got *better* before he brought us here?" Herb posed in confusion.

"Oh, I got a *huge* divorce settlement," Didi clarified, wiping her eyes and composing herself. "I mean, I'm still hurt, or whatever, but I'm filthy fucking rich."

The sympathy evaporated instantly. I rolled my eyes as I shifted my finger toward Vivienne, who immediately shook her head no and crossed her arms.

"*S'il vous plaît?*" I asked as politely as I could.

She sighed a throaty sigh then threw her arms in the air, launching into a string of rapid-fire French that I just barely understood. The others looked at each other, dumbfounded.

"What did she say?" Herb demanded.

"Something about...she was in love with..."

"*Mon producteur*," Vivienne repeated. "Producer. Music. *Alors*, he did not see me that way."

"And she sold her soul to be his wife," I finished.

"Did you get married?" Catalina asked, eagerly.

"*Oui, madame*," she answered with a glow in her eyes. "*Et je me suis retiré.*"

"And she retired," I translated.

"What about Catalina?" Didi snapped, pointing behind me.

"You all know—" she started.

"Yeah, well, most of us have told our stories before this, too, but she's still making us do it again," Didi retorted.

Catalina sighed and eyed Lucian tentatively before beginning her story. "Lucian was nine, and had been battling an aggressive brain tumor since age seven. He'd already had one operation, but they didn't get the whole tumor, and the part they missed grew rapidly. The doctors wanted to do a second surgery after his round of radiation treatment was finished."

She swallowed hard and shifted uncomfortably, hugging her arms in front of her chest. "Um, the risks for the second surgery were higher than the first. There was a chance he could have severe impairment to his vision and speech, not to mention the survival rates of the operation in general. Without the surgery, his prognosis was...he wouldn't have made it to the sixth grade. I just...I couldn't choose. I spent a whole night praying to the Lord to just take it away and I'd do anything. And then I turned elsewhere with my plea," she admitted with shame, tucking her chin to her chest and dropping her eyes to the deck.

Tracie sniffled from the opposite side of the snack table.

"Anyway, I gave consent for the surgery, and when they did the pre-op cat-scan, it was gone," she continued, her voice tight as she looked back up at us. "Just gone. The whole thing. No sign it ever existed. I knew exactly what had happened—who had taken my son's tumor for me. The words I had said when I pleaded to the Devil haunted me almost everyday for the next year. When we ended up here, it didn't take me long at all to figure out why."

I walked to her, placed my hands on her shoulders, and gave her my most sympathetic look.

"That brings us to Lucian," I said slowly, turning away from Catalina, but seeing the look of confusion in her eyes as I did.

Lucian stared back at me with a blank face.

"He-he didn't do anything," Catalina stammered.

"Exactly," I stated, continuing to stare him down.

He didn't flinch.

"Michaela..." Catalina muttered. "What are you saying?"

"I'm saying there is only one person here who didn't actually do anything—didn't make the deal—to get here," I explained as they all stared at me in shocked silence, some of them with gaping jaws and some with widened eyes. "It just so happens to help that we would never suspect him, never even lump him into the list of consideration, because he's a *child*."

"Are you actually insinuating that *my son* is the Devil?" Catalina snapped.

I whipped around to face her again. "I'm so sorry, Catalina, but...I am." I reached out to put a hand on her shoulder again, and she slapped it away and stepped back from me. "It's not your son, though. If I'm right, than this-this person that's been with you the whole time is not your son."

"Then where would my son *be*?" she growled.

"I...I don't know," I muttered. "I guess still in his normal life."

"Without his mother?!" she shouted at me, her face tinged with red and panic. "*Dios mio*—I cannot believe I'm listening to this. From *you*!" She threw her arms toward me in a gesture of anger.

"Catalina, she might be right," Herb declared. "It doesn't make sense why someone would come with you when no one came with any of the rest of us."

"And it's a good disguise," Tracie chimed in timidly. "I mean, he's a child, and your story is so emotional. I never would have questioned it."

"I can't believe this," Catalina scoffed, a frigid, pained laugh plowing forth from her quivering lips like a gust of blizzard wind. "It's because he was involved in my deal!" she tried to reason, desperation filling her voice. "He was a benefactor! Tracie and Bob came together!"

"We both made the deal," Bob replied.

"Some of us had benefactors besides ourselves in the deal, too," Jeric said. "If that were a consideration, our whole crew from the storm would be here."

"They all lived because of *our* deal," Jeff added with a nodded.

"And Vivienne's husband could have come, too, if that were the case," Didi suggested with a shrug.

"You *all* believe this?" Catalina barked. "Seriously?"

"Catalina...it's the first time we've all come even remotely close to agreeing on the plausibility of the Devil's identity," Herb said in a soothing yet regretful tone. "That should tell you something."

She stumbled back and I lunged to steady her from falling, but she wrestled against my touch. Jeric swooped a lawn chair up easily in one hand and slid it under her as she tried to push me off of her, and I let go as soon as it was in place. Collapsing in the chair, she covered her face and started to whimper. "That's my son...he's my son...my son..."

The emotion was as tangible in that moment, as we all watched her, as it had been when she'd told her story. Tracie sniffled again and Jeric, still standing next to the chair, looked down at her with a beard-framed frown. An invisible rope, tethered in my sternum, tugged at me fiercely, willing me toward her to hold her and comfort her but I knew she didn't want it, so I stood my ground against the aching pull.

CLAP!

A singular smack of flesh against flesh sounded behind me. I wheeled around, so quickly I became dizzy in the sway of the boat.

CLAP!

It was Lucian.

CLAP!

His eyes had changed...the expression was no longer blank it was—

CLAP...CLAP...CLAP-CLAP-CLAP!

Devilish.

"Well done, Michaela," Lucian said. "Very well done, indeed. I knew when I told you about my little game on the island I had a limited amount of time before you figured me out."

Didi shrieked and Catalina wailed, and several others gasped. But not me. I stood up straight, puffed my chest, narrowed my eyes, lowered my chin. He smirked.

Catalina wailed in agony behind me. "*No!* God, no!"

I felt like rushing to her, but stayed rooted and kept my stare fixed on the Devil in his disguise. But, it wasn't a second later that she jumped out of her chair and lunged at him, falling to her knees and grabbing him by the shoulders and shaking him.

"Where is my son!?" she shouted in his face. "Where is the real Lucian?!"

"He's in Brooklyn, where you left him," Devil Lucian answered calmly.

"Oh my god..." Catalina gasped and then cried. "Where? With—"

Her voice broke, rendered completely incapable by the constriction of sobs.

"You have a great aunt who lived in Queens," Devil Lucian explained. "I just happened to send her an invite, under your name of course, to Lucian's back-to-school dinner. She was very excited. And when she got to your house, you weren't there. Lucian had been alone all morning. So she stayed."

"Aunt Maria Elena?" Catalina muttered through tears and snot. "She-she's been taking care of him this whole time—what, how long have I been here?"

"Four hundred days," Bob said.

"Damn," Herb muttered.

"That's a long time," I remarked.

"Bob, how do you know this shit?" Herb asked.

"I like numbers..." Bob admitted with a shrug.

"Okay, so if our theory that one day here is one hour in the real world—" Didi started, but Bob cut her off with the answer.

"Sixteen days," he said. "Well, sixteen days, four hours. To be exact."

"Bob," Herb said with a sly grin and cocked brows, "you and Tracie ever been to Vegas?"

"Two weeks?" Catalina gasped. "I've only been gone a little over two weeks?"

Devil Lucian nodded, and I put a hand on her shoulder.

"See, that's not long. And he's been with your Aunt," I whispered. "It's going to be okay."

She took a deep breath and stood up, wiping tears from her cheeks, still shaken but seemingly regaining composure.

Devil Lucian let loose a wicked laugh. It started in his throat, then moved to his nose, then spewed from his ten-year-old lips as a full on maniacal bellow.

"Could you, like, change into the Devil or something," Didi drawled. "The fact that you're a child is a little too Damien's Omen for me right now."

"What? Why are you laughing?" I demanded.

"Oh, oh, oh," he moaned with amusement as he tried to stay his guffaws to speak. "Oh, nothing, it's just...you told her it would be okay!"

He clutched his side and doubled over, his hysterics doubling with him.

We all exchanged a round of nervous glances. Icy dread settled in my intestines.

"We solved your puzzle," I snarled. "Now we're done here...right?"

"Oh, yes, you solved the puzzle," Devil Lucian stated, wiping tears of laughter from his little, innocent-looking face as he stood up straight and locked his eyes on mine. "But, it has to be unanimous. You *all* have to agree on my identity for the game to be over and for you to go home."

I swallowed hard against the nausea that swirled through me when I saw the flicker of victory in his eyes.

"We do!" Didi protested in a pitchy whine.

"We all agree—you fucking told us, you idiot!" Herb shouted.

"Where the fuck is Todd?!" I shouted at him, rage spilling over from my chest into my head and my arms. I grabbed him by the throat, Catalina cried out, Tracie gasped, and Devil Lucian smiled widely. "What the *fuck* did you do?"

"He was pretty torn up about you not coming to see him after lunch..." he taunted, his voice raspy from my strangling grasp. "I just had a special gift delivered to him. To make him feel better."

My circulation stopped dead, the blood and life draining from me. I couldn't feel my pulse and my head spun. "Didi..."

"I'm sorry!" she uttered meekly, her voice squeaking and breaking.

With as much force as I could muster, I threw Devil Lucian

backwards to the hard deck floor, causing another round of instinctive protestation from the mothers who still saw him as a child.

"How *special* was this *gift?*" I roared, towering over him, my voice quaking and rumbling like an active volcano, about to erupt.

"Really fucking special," Devil Lucian answered with wicked grin and arrogant, gloating eyes. "None of that cheap LA street shit he's used to. Even cut it with some other cool shit for him, too. Of course, he didn't know that."

Didn't.

"Fuck!" I yelled. Then I ran.

As fast as my legs could carry me, I sprinted through the cruise ship, just about falling down the stairs, taking the last four in a leap. My ankle buckled when I landed, but I didn't stop, taking the hall in a limping dash until I reached his door. My shoulder rammed into it as I tried to open it, the handle stubbornly refusing to move.

"No!" I screamed. "No! No! Fuck! No!"

The shouts turned to sobs as I started kicking the door with all my strength, each thud and clap of my flip-flopped foot against the door sending hot pain through my whole leg and into my hips and spine.

"Please! Open the door, Todd! *Please!*" I cried, slamming my fist against it over and over until my hand turned flame red and couldn't take the pain anymore. "Damnit...*damnit!*"

I heard footfalls approaching, not at the speed I had taken, but definitely running. Soon, Jeff and Jeric were at my side. I blubbered and panted and threw my hands toward the door in desperation, unable to speak.

With a singular, synchronized stomp of their boots, the door crumpled and wrenched from its hinges, falling into Todd's room. I rushed inside and saw him—sprawled on his back on the floor in a twisted position that looked like he had fallen out of the chair. The baggy sat on the desk, empty.

"Todd," I cried, my entire body shaking as I knelt next to his pale, sweat-covered body, "what the fuck did you do?"

Jeff and Jeric watched from behind me, and I heard more footsteps in the hallway. I didn't look back as I searched for a pulse and looked for signs of breath.

"He's alive, but pulse is weak and irregular," I announced as loud as I could, my voice drained of power. "I need an AED. Or...or a shot of adrenaline. Or something—I don't know what to do! I-I don't..." I positioned the heels of my palms over his sternum, preparing to do chest compressions. Arms locked, I drove downward.

"This ship definitely predates the Automated External Defibrillator, Mickey," Herb stated, his tone ripe with defeat.

"Then something else, damnit!" I shouted, panicking. "Somebody! Fucking do *something*!" I drove down harder. The room filled with the crack of his cartilage and I heard Catalina cry out in the doorway. "Charcoal—or something! Get him to throw up...I-I don't know! I'm not letting him die!"

I kept at the compressions, my elbows and wrists aflame with a burning ache. I looked back at them, all watching me in shocked silence and hopeless despair.

"We're never going to get out of here," I heard Didi say from behind the twins.

"Fuck you, Didi!" I snapped. "Seriously—fuck you! I don't give a fuck about going home right now. He's going to die, you fucking bitch, and it's mostly your fault! So get the fuck out of here!"

"Didi," Herb muttered, "you better go."

"God damnit!" I shrieked at the top of my lungs. My arms were giving out. I couldn't go on much longer and my efforts didn't appear to be doing anything.

How could this be happening? How could he let this happen? He didn't want us dead, did he? I looked around the room as thoughts raced through my head, as loud as the sounds of an actual racetrack. *The Devil didn't want us dead. But he didn't want us to leave...*

"Are you listening?!" I yelled at the ceiling.

"Who are you talking to?" Catalina muttered.

"I will *literally* sell my soul to the Devil to save Todd Arbor Drake's life!" I bellowed. "Do you hear me, Beelzebub?!"

With a poof and a cloud of smoke that smelled of sulfur, he appeared, lying casually on Todd's bed—not in his Lucian disguise, not as an emerald serpent, but in the form that the world was familiar with—horns and all.

"Ooooh, you know I love it when you call me Beelzebub," he cooed, his voice deep and smooth, animated and brimming with inflection, like a radio host. "So, you wanna make a deal?"

"Yes," I grunted, my arms feeling like they would snap at the elbow like a plank in a karate class at any given moment.

"Michaela, no!" Catalina yelled.

"Alright, sugar," the Devil purred like a large feline, his lips pulling back over his gleaming teeth like one, too, "let's make a deal."

CHAPTER 20

THE MONTY HALL PARADOX

"Welcome to Let's Make a Deal, folks! I'm your host, the motherfucking Devil! Alright, Michaela, you can let Todd die and I will let everyone go home, including yourself...or, I will give you what you need to save him, at a price."

"What price?" I snapped.

"You and Todd stay," he murmured, his voice a low taunting growl.

"Michaela—" Catalina started, but I couldn't let her distract me.

She needed to go home. Todd needed to live. I didn't have a choice.

"Fine, deal," I said sharply. "Give me what I need. We stay."

"No..." Catalina gasped from the door.

"Good..." the Devil sneered, his smile going wide. "Alrighty, one magic shot, coming up!"

He snapped his fingers and a shiny little syringe appeared at my side on the floor.

"Does anyone know how to do this?" I asked.

They stared at me in silence, eyes gleaming and jaws hanging loosely from their hinges.

"C'mon, you've never seen Pulp Fiction?" the Devil teased, hopping out of the bed excitedly. "This is my favorite scene! I mean, he's no Uma Thurman...but you're pretty hot."

I rolled my eyes. "Shut up." I took a deep breath to try and steady my aching, trembling hands.

Catalina's muffled crying grew louder and I tried to push it out of my head. I ripped Todd's shirt open. His skin was white as a sheet and I shuddered.

"No, don't listen to him!" Catalina ejected. "Not in his chest. That's movie bullshit. Generally speaking, poking a hole in the heart is a big no-no."

I looked over my shoulder at Catalina. "Where?" I pleaded, my throat and eyes hot.

"What is it?" she asked, tears streaming down her flushed cheeks.

I peered at the side of the syringe. "Naloxone."

"That's...that's for heroin. It will stop the affects of an overdose. The thigh, like an epinephrine shot? Or, maybe...maybe the arm?" she stammered. "I-I don't know."

"Door number one, door number two," the Devil hummed over my shoulder. "Door number one, door number two..."

"Shove it, Satan," I snapped.

"Just pick a muscle," Catalina squeaked. "Either one should work!"

"Catalina," I said softly, positioning the syringe over Todd's leg, unable to look her in the eyes.

"What?"

"Thank you," I whispered. I managed to look at her for a brief moment. "Hold your son tight tonight, okay?"

"Michaela—"

With all the strength I could muster, I stabbed the syringe through

Todd's jeans and into his thigh, plunging the liquid down through the needle. The dose completely administered, I pulled it out and collapsed on the floor in a heap next to him, each ragged, exhausted breath like frostbite in the sweltering, fiery caverns of my lungs. Adrenaline coursed through every inch of me, making me nauseous. I could feel it oozing from my skin and trying to escape by way of my throat.

Eery quiet fell across the room, spilling in from the hall like a wintery chill. I shivered as I sat up and looked around to find that everyone was gone. Vanished. Even the Devil.

Gone. *Just gone*, Catalina's voice filled my head, as if she were there still, murmuring in my ear. *No sign it ever existed.*

I sat there, in the discomforting silence, hugging my knees and holding back tears. I had no idea how long the naxolone would take, and every passing moment made my skin crawl with anxiety that it didn't work —that I messed it up and I gave up my shot to go home for nothing. Relief flooded my chest when I finally heard a gasp and grunt next to me.

I spun on my rear to face him as he attempted to hoist himself up to sitting. He tried to push himself up with his right arm, but he winced and yelped in pain as it buckled under him and he clutched his chest.

"Fuck...what the hell happened?" Todd groaned.

As gently as I could, I helped him sit up. "Your gift had a little extra *giftiness* to it this time. I'm pretty sure I fucked up your sternum. Sorry."

"Wow, that bad, huh?" he asked, his voice feeble and hoarse.

"You have no fucking idea…"

"Did you also rip my shirt open?" he asked with a faint smirk, trying to infuse some humor and flirting into his tone, but he was so weak, so shaken, it wasn't very successful.

"I thought I'd have to inject something in your heart—"

"What the fuck?!"

"—but it turns out that's just Hollywood bullshit. I did it in your leg. Naxolone."

"The fuck is that?"

"For heroine overdoses," I answered.

"Oh, that was the extra giftiness," he muttered, dropping his eyes in shame.

"Yep," I replied.

"How in the world did you…?" he started, then he grimaced and clutched his chest again.

"I, uh…I made a deal," I croaked.

"Fuck. *Mickey*…" he exhaled.

"Everyone is gone," I uttered, my voiced strangled. "It's just you and me. That was the deal. We figured it all out—I figured it out. And he was going to send us all home if I just let you die. Or, if I saved you, we both had to stay."

"Jesus Christ."

"So here we are."

"I think you should have let me go," Todd murmured.

I slapped him in the arm.

"Ow! Ow...ow," he whimpered.

"I think you mean *thank you*, Mickey!" I shouted. "Thank you for giving up your life, maybe your only chance to go home, to save my life after I royally fucked everything up for everyone on this ship! I think *that's* what you mean, Todd!"

"Yes!" He grabbed my shoulders and squeezed them tightly, his face pulling in agony as he did. "Yes, that is what I mean. Thank you. Really, I just...I don't deserve it. I don't deserve what you gave up, and I have no way to repay you."

I grabbed his face in my hands and looked him dead in the eyes. "You wanna repay me?" I snapped. He nodded, his eyes filled with apology and glistening with a sheen of sadness and shame. "Don't touch that shit ever again."

He nodded again and swallowed audibly. "Okay."

"Okay," I whispered.

His thumbs massaged my arms and I finally broke, sobs spilling out of me uncontrollably, heaving my entire body as they did. Todd pulled me into him and I dropped my forehead onto his shoulder as the despair I'd been bottling took me completely in its grips and throes.

"I'm so sorry, Mickey," Todd whispered into my hair, rubbing my back with one hand and stroking my arm with the other. "I am so, so sorry..."

I don't know how long I cried, but I know it was long enough to feel like I'd never stop. Long enough to make me feel sick and light-headed. Long enough that the porthole changed from blue to orange to lavender-gray.

After I finally managed to compose myself, I helped Todd into his bed, and, knowing I would never fall asleep in the desolate static of my room, lied down next to him.

"Maybe it's supposed to be this way," Todd murmured, grabbing my hand under the sheets. "Just you and me, I mean."

"Maybe," I sighed. "Maybe it is."

Warmth against my face alerted my eyelids to open. Vision muddled and eyes fogged by sleep, I strained to focus on the little square of red on my bedside table.

I shot up and rubbed my eyes vigorously.

My bedside table.

Mine. Not the cheap, ugly one in my cabin on the cruise ship that I would have loved to swing a sledgehammer at, if I could have found one. Mine in my apartment. My just-as-cheap IKEA nightstand, with my little vintage clock and my stack of unread books.

I cocked my head as my vision cleared.

The little red square had my name written on it, propped against the base of the lamp. I knew what it was—who it was from. I ripped it open, heart pounding nervously, but a smile starting to creep across my face in spite of my anxiety. I was *off that cruise ship*. I was *home*. That was a start...even if he was going to throw another curve ball at me.

ALRIGHT, SO THAT DOOR HAD A PRIZE! THE PRIZE WAS YOU BECOMING A NOBLE, MORAL COMPASS CARRYING, LITTLE GOODY TWO SHOES, AND I AIN'T TRYIN' TO FUCK WITH YOU LIKE THAT, AS THEY SAY IN THE MODERN SLANG.

ANYWAY, IT WAS FUN, MY SWEET MANGO. ENJOY YOUR NEXT SET OF DOORS.

LOVE,

BEE

My next set of doors? I wondered. I didn't have much time to decipher his code, my phone buzzing eagerly on the pillow next to me. I grabbed and looked at the screen,

A text message from Rafe: *Look, I'm not sure what last night was about, but..I noticed your car was still at Mozzarella Mitch's. Anyway, if the cruise was a cover for bolting, I won't be upset. I just want us to be honest with each other.*

I took a sharp inhale. It had only been a day...of course. I could still make it work with Rafe. I could forget the whole thing ever happened.

No sign it ever existed, I thought.

I texted back: *Sure. When and where?*

Well, on the off-chance you were home, I have coffee and bagels. I'm at your door.

I gasped and choked on my own saliva as a result. A knock sounded at the door and my stomach flipped. I jumped out of bed and rushed to answer it, only just realizing I probably looked a mess right as I laid eyes on him, perfect and polished and holding a tray of hot coffee cups in one hand and a brown paper bag in the other.

"Oh my god, you're actually here," he said in shock.

"Yes, I..." I didn't know how to explain my cruise with the Devil, and I was partially convinced that it would come out as one of his bad jokes anyway. "Look, I-I had some stuff that I had to deal with. I was just, um...too embarrassed to talk about it."

"That's okay," Rafe said. "I understand. I just...I wanted to make sure it wasn't because of me. I mean, we rushed into it—I know—but, I am not like that. And I want to do things the right way. If you want to, I mean."

He was gorgeous, and successful, and he wanted me. And I felt nothing. I pictured him throwing the bagels and the coffee on my breakfast counter and swooping me up in those sculpted arms, and taking me back to bed. And I felt nothing...

"Rafe, I am so sorry, I—"

"Oh."

"It's not you! You're wonderful, and you're going to make someone really happy. It's just not going to be me. I'm sorry, I—you can come in and have your coffee, but I have to go check on someone."

"What?" he asked, his face scrunched in confusion.

"God, I am so sorry," I said. "But, I have to go see someone. It's really important. You're welcome to stay—"

"Okay, look, I think I should just go. Here's the latte I got you, and some bagels," he said curtly.

"I really couldn't take them," I refused.

"Fine, whatever." He turned to leave.

"Actually...actually, can I have that latte?" I asked meekly, pouting my lips and squinting my eyes in apology.

He yanked the cup out of the tray and shoved it into my hand. "Bye, Mickey."

"Thank you," I whispered as he stormed away. "Sorry..."

As soon as he was out of sight, I rushed to my laptop, fueling up with a few swigs of the latte as I brought up Google.

Todd Drake news, I typed into the search bar.

Comedian Todd Drake set to kick off tour in Los Angeles after mysterious disappearance

LA'S HOTTEST NEW COMEDIAN, TODD ARBOR DRAKE, WHO DISAPPEARED FOR EIGHT DAYS ON THE EVE OF A HIGHLY ANTICIPATED NORTH AMERICAN TOUR, HAS RETURNED TO HIS BURBANK HOME, HIS PUBLICISTS ANNOUNCED THIS MORNING. DRAKE, RECENTLY NAMED ONE OF ROLLING STONE MAGAZINE'S TOP TEN YOUNG COMEDIANS TO WATCH BASED ON THE WILD AND SEEMINGLY OVERNIGHT SUCCESS OF HIS FIRST STAND-UP ALBUM, *ARBOR DAY,* PLANS TO COMPLETE HIS TOUR AS SCHEDULED, TACKING THE CITIES HE MISSED IN HIS AS YET UNEXPLAINED ABSENCE ONTO THE END OF THE TOUR AND OFFERING FULL REFUNDS FOR THOSE WHO WANT IT.

FANS AND MEDIA SPECULATED THAT DRUGS, NAMELY COCAINE--WHICH DRAKE HAS BEEN VOCAL ABOUT STRUGGLING WITH IN HIS ROUTINES--MAY HAVE PLAYED A PART IN HIS VANISHING ACT. DRAKE IS EXPECTED TO RELEASE A STATEMENT TODAY, HOWEVER, THOSE WITH TICKETS TO SEE HIM LIVE CAN PROBABLY EXPECT TO

HEAR PARTS OF THE STORY STRAIGHT FROM THE COMEDIAN'S
MOUTH, STARTING TONIGHT.

I smiled as I opened a new tab and searched for flights. The next available was in two hours. With a good Uber driver, I could make it. Being last minute, it cost a pretty penny, but I reminded myself my student loans were paid. Then I reminded myself I'd likely be out of a job if I did this. Ran off, *again*.

It didn't matter. No time to hesitate. I paid for the ticket, the last one left on the flight, hammering my info into the keyboard. When it was confirmed, I slammed my laptop shut and threw it in a messenger bag with my wallet, makeup bag, a toothbrush and toothpaste, and a change of clothes. I pulled on a pair of tennis shoes and scheduled an Uber on my phone while I brushed my hair and tied it back in a twist and swished some mouthwash around and spit.

The driver got me to the airport with just enough time for check-in and security. I ran up to my gate just as they started to board. My nerves got the better of me for the first half of the non-stop flight, so I caved and ordered a white wine to take some of the edge off. It was a long flight to the coast, and I spent most of it in my own head, despite several attempts to zone out on the in-flight movie.

When the plane finally landed, I looked up the address I needed in the White Pages on my phone, my hands shaky and sweaty, my pulse racing. During Uber ride number two, my heart never let up on its insistent drumming and my brain continued to fill with doubt and uncertainty.

What the fuck am I doing? I repeated in my head, over and over. *What the fuck am I doing?*

The car stopped in front of the house and I stepped out, feeling like I'd melt to a puddle of anxiety on the concrete. Taking a deep breath, I practiced what I was going to say.

"I know it was fast, and...I know it was short. And I know that it's probably crazy that I'm here, but, I realized that I'm never going to be able to forget that fucking cruise because I don't want to. I don't want to forget you. I don't want to forget you and me together. And, I don't want that to be the end of it, either," I muttered, pacing up and down the sidewalk in front of the house. Pigeons scurried out of my path, then back to their positions when I'd pivot, then back out of my path when I'd turn and pace toward them again.

"I want to get to know you. I want to go out on real dates with you and make plans with you and...I want to say good morning and good night to you—okay, Mickey, this is getting cheesy real fast. Just go."

I marched up the steps with one more inhale, as deep as I could take it, and knocked on the door as I pushed my exhale through my lips like I were blowing out a candle.

Footsteps sounded in syncopation with my fiercely beating heart and it practically somersaulted into my throat when the door flew open.

Everything I thought I was going to say vanished into the air between us. All I could muster was a self-conscious smile, a shrug, and a squeaky "Hi."

I waited with bated breath for a response, swallowing hard against my doubt.

Then came a smile. Then a tilt of the head. Then that familiar voice...

"Michaela?"

A NOTE FROM THE AUTHOR

I really hope you enjoyed this crazy story I concocted, and I definitely hope it made you laugh. If you want to join me for future journeys in humorous fiction, I invite you to visit my website at WWW.JESSICABENOISTYOUNG.COM and sign up for updates on new releases.

This book would not have materialized into the book you're holding today if it weren't for some incredible people and I'd like to give a few shout outs to them.

A big thank you to Kelly, my best friend and favorite beta reader, whose "send me more" emails are the best encouragement I know of for a writer.

To the original Stripper Squad - Olivia, Milena, Mia, Lacey, Paula - thank you for all your support and for all the big (and the little!) things you do every day to help me bring all of this to life.

santa clara
county
library district

Renewals: (800) 471-0991

www.sccl.org

70088721R00165

Made in the USA
Lexington, KY
08 November 2017